I LIED TO YOU ABOUT EVERYTHING

A Myrtle Jenson Mystery

M. MALENGA

Copyright © 2018 Mubita Malenga

All rights reserved.

ISBN: 0578407876
ISBN-978-0-578-40787-6

DEDICATION

Mother.
Sisters.
Brother.
Father.

I LIED TO YOU ABOUT EVERYTHING

A Myrtle Jenson Mystery

CHAPTER 1

It was a freezing night in February when the big train crash happened. The cabin lights dim shortly after the last boarding call and most of the passenger cars are whisper quiet as the locomotive pulls out of the station. Restless passengers settle into their seats and attempt to get some sleep. This is the last train out of town tonight. This trip is the equivalent of a red-eye flight. The melodic rumble of the train wheels rolling over the tracks puts the riders into a soothing trance and rocks them to sleep. The crew is relieved the train boarded all its passengers and baggage without incident or major delay. Tonight's train is filled with last-minute travelers trying to get to their holiday destinations. Among the passengers this evening are two young women, Tanya and Tiffany. These two travelers are fed up with small town living and have made up their minds to do something about it. Talk is cheap and easy, acting is hard. These two strangers each decided on their own that they could either spend their lives complaining about their situation or do something about it. Neither one of the women has ever lived anywhere else besides Viewgrove but the fear of being stuck there all their lives was stronger than their fear of leaving. Too many times they had heard friends complain and talk a big game about leaving town only to have something happen that derails their plans. Some friends got married, had children, or both. Other friends fell into the rut of trying to earn a daily living and put their dreams of leaving on hold. Some were obligated to take over the family business from their aging parents, essentially killing any hopes of them ever leaving town.

The weather on this night borders on hazardous. It is the middle of winter in Viewgrove and old man winter feels like showing off. The overnight temperature is in the low teens. The town experiences all four seasons and is no stranger to winter. The Viewgrove winters are usually mild, nothing like tonight, this is a rare winter storm. After much inspection and deliberation, the train is cleared to travel, had this been an airplane the flight would have been delayed or even canceled. Not even a winter storm like this can dampen the spirits of the two young travelers on board. The adrenaline of finally leaving this small-town blind them to the dangers of traveling in a storm like this. It has been said the youth is wasted on the young, but youth does allow for more risk to be taken without fear of the consequences. In the case of these two travelers, their hopes and dreams are keeping them warm. Meanwhile, there are plenty of other passengers on the train who are scared to death to travel in this weather and will not be able to relax the whole trip. A sizeable number of passengers canceled their tickets or rescheduled them for a different date. The train is nowhere near as packed as it normally would be. The weather is a huge contributing factor but also this is a red-eye trip. After a few uneventful miles into the trip, the remaining passengers do settle down and get comfortable for the night. The train crew walks through the quiet train cars to make sure everybody is situated. Most of the passengers have dozed off to sleep already. The two young travelers are too excited to sleep. At some point during the night both women find themselves in the Observation Car, it is the only car still open, the Dining Car is closed and will not reopen for several hours. Even though they both live in Viewgrove and are of similar age they have never met each other. Since they are the only two people in the Observation Car, Tanya and Tiffany eventually strike up a conversation. They start off talking about where they are headed and to their surprise learn they are headed to the same place. The conversation soon switches to their experiences in Viewgrove. It is rare in a town that size for two people around the same age to have never met. It made more sense after one of the ladies revealed she was homeschooled her whole life by the foster parents who adopted her. The two women get along swimmingly and talk and laugh for hours. They resemble each other physically and could possibly pass as sisters.

One of the young ladies just starts to doze off to sleep but is awakened by the searing sound of metal collapsing and bending against its will. The first initial jolt is followed by a frightening noise. The violent jolt sends terrified passengers and their belongings bouncing about the train cars. The crumple sounds are followed by a loud screeching sound as the train slows to a halt. The young traveler scrambles to her feet while also bracing for another possible collision. A power outage plunges the Observation Car into total darkness. The heavy scent of a toxic metallic vapor hangs in the air. The other young lady that she spent the night in conversation with is nowhere to be found. She calls out for her, but her voice is scratchy from being asleep and the metallic air causes her to cough when she inhales to breathe. Again, she calls out, this time a little stronger, but there is still no reply. Her eyes have not adjusted to the darkness, but it appears there is nobody else in the train car. She turns her focus toward the soft glow of the emergency lights cutting through the darkness. Pushing some loose debris off her, she gingerly tiptoes toward the glow being extra careful not to step on anything that may have fallen over during the melee. The young woman peers through the train window into the darkness outside. The soft glow of lights is radiating from the emergency lights on several train cars that have derailed. The train going around a curve makes the rear train cars visible from the ones ahead. There is twisted metal and pieces of track spewed all along the countryside along with warning sirens blaring in the distance. With focus, she can make out the outline of several injured people laying on the ground, possibly train staff although she cannot be sure. The young lady attempts to open the window, but it is jammed shut, the frame is most likely bent and locking it in place. She makes her way to the door that connects to the next train car but some obstacle on the other side must be blocking it because it will not slide open. Unable to help, she can only watch as the fallen and wounded victims suffer outside in the frigid temperature. Help does finally arrive, but it is too late to save a lot of them. It is the most tragic day in Viewgrove history.

CHAPTER 2

The class action lawsuits and the vast number of settlements resulting from the train accident bankrupt the local railroad company. It is years later and due to some new investors, the Viewgrove train line is back up and running. The surrounding area newspapers labeled the crash as The Great Train Catastrophe. The train derailment scarred the town's residents for many years, many residents lost loved ones that day. To make matters worse, the train company had to layoff their whole workforce due to going bankrupt. There were so many civil lawsuits filed in addition to the class action suit that the company was buried in litigation fees. Most residents felt the train company was negligent in allowing the train to run that night and held them responsible. In the months that followed, parts of the train tracks became overgrown and fell into disrepair from sheer neglect. The part of the rail where the accident happened became a makeshift memorial. Some people in town believed a train would never run on those tracks again. There was some talk of turning the wreckage site into an official memorial by commissioning a statue, or park, or wall plaque. The plans, however, were never finalized because no one could agree on what type of memorial it should be. There was also genuine concern over whether a memorial was the best use of the town's limited budget. Viewgrove is not a rich community by any means, there are a few wealthy families but no millionaires living in town. No private donor had stepped forward to pay for the potential memorial, so it would be left to the taxpayers to foot the bill. Time heals wounds and popular opinion changes as new issues arise. There was a small but growing band of locals who were championing the 'Build the Memorial' movement. The contested battle lasted several years, but in the end, the town passed the bill to build a memorial to the victims of the great train wreck. Just as construction was due to begin on the memorial there was another big town announcement. The town's leadership held an emergency vote and voted to restore the train line. The memorial would still be built but at another site to be voted on later. Town leadership felt it was time Viewgrove reconnected with the rest of the world. The town desperately needed new sources of revenue. The most common belief around at that time, mainly held by the younger folks, was that more commerce would come to Viewgrove if it was more accessible to the outside world. Increased contact with the surrounding areas would create more local opportunities and decrease the number of young people migrating away. This increased connection theory did not go unchallenged. There was opposition to this line of thought. Would the culture of their town be destroyed by the influx of tourists and outside business interests?

One of the many people grateful that the Train Bill passed is Tanya. Without the train, her current travel to Viewgrove would be decidedly more arduous. Tanya snaps open her eyes and a panic comes over her as her mind scrambles to determine where she is. Her eyes dart around in search of something familiar which she can use to gather her bearings. She tries to steady her breathing by telling herself she is okay.

"You're okay, you're okay" she whispers to herself as her heart slowly stops racing.

Tanya is now aware she is moving, the trees zooming by outside the window come into focus, and now she remembers everything. She is on the train on her way into Viewgrove and must have dozed off. The view out of the window does not appear to have changed so it makes it hard for her to tell how long she has been asleep. It happened again, she always seems to have the same dream whenever she rides a train now. Every time she is transported back to the night of the big train disaster. If she were to diagnose herself, she would say she is exhibiting signs of post-traumatic stress disorder or PTSD. The nightmares and anxiety she experiences are both symptoms of PTSD. The "Big Winter Derailment" is what the Viewgrove Gazette had labeled it. The personal nightmare is what Tanya had labeled it. There was so much destruction that night and so many injured passengers. It is hard to get images like that out of your mind. The nightmares had become so frequent that Tanya had made it a point to avoid riding trains, but this was the most cost-efficient way to get to Viewgrove. Her friends had convinced her with statistics that avoiding trains was silly.

In their defense, she had not disclosed to them how serious the PTSD issue had become for her. So here she is, safe and sound and on her way into town. Well, since she is up she decides to purchase something to drink onboard the train. The bottled water she packed could quench her thirst but will do nothing for her nerves. Tanya decides to head over to the Dining Car for something more interesting to drink. The train trip is almost over, perhaps a small drink would relax her. She walks up and takes a seat at the bar. The bartender acknowledges her before finishing up with the only other patron at the bar. The bartender gives them their change before walking over to Tanya with a wide friendly smile.

"Hello, what can I make for you today?"

"Hello, give me a moment", replies Tanya.

Tanya thinks for a moment before ordering a glass of her favorite Chardonnay. Those buttery, smooth, tropical fruit tones are exactly what a situation like this calls for. "Yes, definitely the Chardonnay". The bartender is sorry to inform her they do not carry the wine she has ordered. An embarrassed look comes over his face as he must admit to her that the train caters more to the beer, cognac, and whiskey crowd. They do not sell a lot of chardonnay, so therefore they do not keep it in stock.

"Would you like to try what I consider the unofficial chardonnay of beers?"

The offer makes Tanya laugh but she still declines it. Admittedly the bartender is kind of charming. Suddenly, she becomes concerned about her appearance. She has just awoken from a nightmare and has not looked in the mirror to see if her curly hair is a mess. It is too late now anyway, although she still tries to catch glimpses of herself in the back-wall mirror of the bar and fix her hair when he is not looking. "I'll tell you what, I can either make you something I think you will like just as much or I do have this White Zinfandel?"

"I'm not sure I could trust whatever you came up with from behind that limited bar."

This time the bartender laughs, a customer with a sense of humor makes his job more enjoyable. Based on the circumstances he really cannot blame her for the comment. "Touché." The bartender makes Tanya a deal. If she does not tell all her online followers about the limited selection at the bar, she can have the wine for free. "It's a deal", replies Tanya. To her surprise, she spends the rest of the train ride at the bar flirting with the bartender and sipping her wine.

CHAPTER 3

There is nobody to meet Tanya on the train platform, so she wheels her luggage through the station and out onto the main street. Although she is not expecting anybody to meet her at the train station, it would have gone a long way toward easing her nerves. She inhales deeply, the main part of the journey is done, this is the home stretch. The air feels crisp and fresh, just as she remembered. Viewgrove still feels like a small town to her, is it possible they have any of those transportation services you can order through a phone app? Just as she pulls her phone out to check, a local taxi pulls up in front of the station. The taxi barely comes to a complete stop before the driver jumps out and asks if she needs a ride. Tanya peers into the cab looking for anything to indicate he is a real driver. Her eyes eventually come across a license number posted in the front passenger seat. It seems legit enough, so she takes a chance. The taxi driver seems oblivious to his potential passenger's hesitation. He swiftly makes his way around to the back of the car and opens the trunk. Tanya takes a step back at the sound of the trunk opening.

"Your bags Miss?", asks the driver, now wondering why his fare is so jumpy.

"Oh, yes, of course," she answers, embarrassed by her response.

The driver points at the luggage still in her tight grasp while locking eye contact with her. Only after receiving a nod of approval does he cautiously lift the red rolling suitcase into the trunk. Tanya has never noticed how many people have red luggage until she took this trip, she always thought her shade of red was unique until today. After closing the trunk, the driver makes his way to open the back door only to find his passenger has already let herself in. "Where to ma'am?" Tanya unlocks her phone and reads the address to the driver. "Oh, I know where that is, I'll get you there in no time", volunteers the cheerful driver as he puts the car in drive and pulls out into traffic without checking to see if it was even safe to do so.

"That's a lovely area, do you get to spend a lot of time there?"

"No", answers Tanya.

"Not the chatty type huh?" replies the driver.

"I'm just tired from traveling", she replies.

The truth is she is exhausted from traveling. She is not trying to be rude to the taxi driver, but she is far too distracted with what to expect when she reaches her destination to engage in small talk. At least she no longer considers him dangerous. He seems like a nice enough guy just trying to earn a living. Tanya is used to traveling in ride-share vehicles that offer passengers free water and snacks to encourage passengers to give a good rating. This cab is very basic but thankfully has heat. Tanya is content to watch the scenery of the town roll by through the taxi window. Viewgrove is more built up than she remembers, and it reminds her how long she has been away. Perhaps she will have a chance to visit her old neighborhood and reminisce.

It is the middle of the morning when the taxi cab pulls up into the driveway of their destination. "Here we are ma'am", announces the driver. Tanya looks out the window in amazement. The home is quite grand, it is a Colonial style home. The house is two stories with a porch in front. She recognizes it as a colonial because the front door is centered between the four windows and the top level has five windows. The front door has a decorative crown and the overhanging eaves display classical detailing. Looks like all those hours spent watching those house hunting shows paid off, she is quite proud of herself for identifying the style of home. The trunk flies open, and the sound of a suitcase being placed on the ground can be heard in the background. Tanya exits the vehicle and pays the taxi driver. Before she can ask another question, the cab pulls around and is off just as quickly as it arrived, off to collect another taxi fare she assumes. So much for waiting to verify this is the right address. Then again, he could have asked her almost anything at that moment and she probably would not remember him doing it. Who is to say if he did ask her if she wanted him to wait or not? Tanya pulls up the retractable handle on her suitcase and tugs it behind her toward the front door of the house. Her eyes light up at the sight of the front porch display.

The porch is beautifully decorated in a fall harvest theme. The impressive display is composed of pumpkins, pinecones, gourds, corn stalks, fall foliage, wreaths, bales of hay, and even some agricultural tools. Out of the corner of her eye, something else catches her attention. There is a figure sitting on the front porch gently rocking back and forth in a rocking chair, perhaps a scarecrow or some other realistic decoration. The fall sky is overcast, and the covered porch casts a shadow that makes it difficult to identify any facial features from a distance. The closer she gets to the front door, the easier it is to make out the figure on the porch. She pastes on her friendliest smile and waves at the figure on the porch. The figure does not wave back or acknowledge her presence. The nervous feeling from earlier returns to her stomach. Is it possible they forgot she is coming today? Did the figure on the front porch not recognize her? Tanya makes her way up the front steps and peers over her right shoulder toward the figure perched in the chair toward the end of the porch. She carefully sets her luggage down beside the front door and takes a cautious step toward the figure. Now that she is closer it is clear to see that the figure is sitting in a rocking chair with a hand-knitted throw blanket covering the lower half of their body. At this close range, she can hear the creaking noise caused by the bottom of the chair rubbing against the wooden porch. At this close range, it is also clear the rocking motion is caused by the occasional gust of wind and not by the chair's occupant. A gust would push on the back of the chair forcing it to slowly rock and return to a standstill long enough for the next breeze to push through and rock it again. Tanya touches the hand poking out from under the knitted throw to wake them up. The hand feels cool to the touch. As she reaches around the wrist to feel for a pulse, she is startled as the hand suddenly reaches up and grabs her. She shrieks and freaks out. Her reflex is to yank her hand back. Her initial attempt to free herself is unsuccessful which only panics her more. She is locked in a tight grip that will not let go.

CHAPTER 4

Myrtle Mae Jenson's day starts, unlike most others. She wakes up at 6 o'clock in the morning on the train heading into Viewgrove. She is returning from a leisure trip to Florida with her girlfriends. Myrtle is an experienced traveler and it is one of her favorite things to do. As soon as the train stops she grabs her polka dot patterned rolling suitcase, exits the train platform, and heads toward her car. She has recently adopted a new fitness routine and is trying her best not to let anything pull her away from that path. Myrtle likes to think of it more of a slight change in lifestyle choices rather than a fitness routine. A week ago, she mentioned making some lifestyle changes to some of the ladies in the water aerobics class at the YMCA. During the same class, one of her girlfriends suggests to Myrtle that she may want to consider going vegan. Vegan sounded a little too extreme for Myrtle's taste, despite her girlfriend stressing all the positives. This lady converted to a vegan lifestyle two years ago and it helped her body to feel a lot better. As a last effort, this girlfriend suggests a two-week vegan challenge. The vegan challenge allows Myrtle a test run to equip her to make an informed decision. There is just no talking Myrtle into the vegan lifestyle though, however, she does agree to give up coffee, soda, and processed food for two weeks. The biggest challenge for her will be giving up her morning coffee. Her girlfriends from the water aerobics class notice the difference right away, Myrtle is a lot grumpier lately. They attribute it to caffeine withdraw and cannot wait until the challenge is over. The morning cup of coffee that has been part of her morning routine for so long is now replaced with a fruit and vegetable smoothie. Myrtle has no trouble finding her car because she parks in the same spot whenever she takes a trip. Viewgrove is a very low crime town so she has no reservations about leaving her car at the train station. On these types of trips, she finds it easier to leave her car than to wait for somebody to pick her up. She throws her luggage in the trunk of her car before heading down the street toward her home.

Once at home, Myrtle resists the temptation to stretch out on the couch and take a nap. She slept on the train, but it is not what she would consider good sleep. Plus, there is her determination to stick to her new lifestyle program, a program that includes a daily walk around the neighborhood for exercise. A week ago, she would have been reaching for her largest coffee mug while going through the mail but today she is reaching for the blender that she now leaves out on the kitchen counter. The ingredients are simple, 1 cup seedless green grapes, 1 cup packaged baby spinach, ½ cup ice, and ¼ cup coconut milk. The ingredients are tossed into the jar where they are blended until they become a smooth green frothy smoothie. To her surprise, the smoothie does not taste as bad as it looks. Myrtle sips on her freshly-blended breakfast smoothie while watching the local news morning broadcast. She glances longingly at her trusty old coffee maker that now shares counter space with the blender. When Myrtle retired from her job as a school psychologist, she received a new modern coffee maker that makes a cup-at-a-time as a gift. "No need to throw away her old perfectly working coffee machine", she thought, "if something ever happens to it then I'll watch the video or whatever to learn how to use that new one." In the meantime, the new machine just sits in her kitchen cabinet unopened. Davina Roberts is a local reporter with the Viewgrove Gazette who sometimes appears as a special news correspondent on the local news broadcast. Myrtle has enjoyed following the rise of Davina's career. When she first moved to Viewgrove she would skip the local news because she did not find it very interesting. Now that she has lived in town for some time she has become accustomed to the local ways and the local news has suddenly become more interesting. Once you know the rules, the game becomes a lot more interesting.

Myrtle finishes her smoothie and heads out for her daily walk around the neighborhood. She likes to exercise at this hour because the air is crisp, and it is not too hot outside. During her walk, she thinks about her day, any upcoming decisions, or life in general. Today her mind wanders back to how she even happens to be in Viewgrove. Myrtle moved to town for a fresh start after her long-time husband was killed. She learned everything there is to know about solving crimes in hopes of putting her husband's murderer behind bars. Before her husband's murder, Myrtle knew very little about crime solving or investigative police work. After the murder, she made it her personal mission to become an expert. She took classes, volunteered at police stations, and went on several ride-alongs. Once the affected parties calmed down they would often ask the officer who the silver-haired lady was? Myrtle has spent a career as a psychologist, so she has excellent communication skills. On slow nights on patrol Myrtle would pass the time by helping officers with their personal problems. The squad car would turn into a mobile therapy couch. The word quickly got out and officers would compete to have Myrtle ride along with them. On the nights a ride-along was not available, Myrtle watched documentaries, and read books on the art of crime solving. In retirement age, she has transformed herself and learned a new trade. Even though it is a steep learning curve, the skills she had sharpened during her career as a school psychologist in the big city transfer well to crime solving.

After her husband's murder case, Myrtle left the big city and moved to Viewgrove for a new start. Old habits are hard to break. Myrtle got selected to jury duty on a few local criminal cases and then she got selected for jury duty on a high-profile case from a neighboring city. The case was too infamous in its own city, so it was moved to Viewgrove in hopes of assembling an impartial jury. It appears that retired school psychologists are popular with both attorneys and law enforcement. Attorneys love to select her for jury panels and law enforcement officers love to select her for character profiles. Her reputation for analyzing crime scene data and criminal motives grew. With the recognition came some less than factual reporting. There was an early story written in the local paper in which the reporter referred to Myrtle as a retired psychiatrist. Ever since that story published, everybody always thinks she is a retired psychiatrist, so she finds herself having to constantly correct people.

Over time Myrtle has become somewhat of a local celebrity at the courthouse. However, she does not take the local fame too seriously because her focus is helping people by uncovering the truth. One of her biggest fears is the fame will go to her head. She fears the fame could cause her to become careless, she may miss a clue, and a guilty person will get away with a crime. Myrtle feels the weight of the responsibility every time she serves on a jury.

CHAPTER 5

Tanya barely has time to process the situation before her thoughts are interrupted by the sound of sirens. Her mind tries to process if those are Police or Ambulance sirens? She is knocked back to reality by the sight of Police cruisers with lights flashing. They pull up to the property in time to catch Tanya on the porch. Also, on the porch is a dead body. The Police are responding to a prowler and break-in call.

"Police! Freeze ma'am! Put your hands up high where we can see them."

A frightened Tanya fumbles her words while she tries her best to explain herself to the hulking police officer barking instructions in her direction. Her voice is weak and fragile, and her throat feels dry. The officers do not understand what has happened here, but once she tells them everything will be okay, right? She takes a step forward; her thought is to move closer to the officer, so he can hear her better.

"Put your hands up and don't move!"

Tanya stops dead in her tracks. She initially felt things would be fine if she could just explain but now she is not so sure. Now she is feeling more and more nervous about her welfare. This situation feels like it could escalate quickly. She tries to plead her case again, but it only becomes more painful and less loud or clearer. The attempts to yell back are futile and only result in coughing attacks. A hurt and frustrated Tanya breaks down into tears as she complies with the officer's instructions. She stops moving, stops trying to explain herself, and holds her hands up as high as she can get them. A concerned elderly woman attempts to exit the home through the front door but is quickly ordered by Police to stay in the house until the scene is secure.

Leading the Police response is Officer Casper "Zeus" Chaplin. Although Officer Chaplin earned the nickname in his younger days, it still applies today. The reason they called him Zeus becomes obvious once he enters a room. Zeus Chaplin is a rather large individual who clearly is dedicated to his physical fitness. Zeus was a bodybuilder in his younger years before joining the Police force. At the height of his competition days, he stood 6 feet 5 inches and weighed a hulking 270 pounds. A young Casper Chaplin impressed the judges with his 29-inch thighs, 59-inch chest and a 34-inch waist. His most popular pose was when he flexed his well-oiled 21-inch chocolate biceps on stage to the crowd's delight. He was quite successful at it and went on to capture several amateur bodybuilding titles. He hates to brag about his old bodybuilding prowess but if you buy him a few drinks he may share a bodybuilding story or five with you. Those competition days are long behind him.

Zeus Chaplin was well on his way to a professional bodybuilding career when his life changed course. People who were involved in the sport at that time remember him well. He was a young man, just a few years removed from his high school graduation. His dream was to make it as a professional bodybuilder, at that time this was his only focus. Zeus supported himself by working odds and ends jobs like most young people do while chasing their dream. When he was not at work he was in the gym working on his size and symmetry. This was not a glamorous life by any stretch, without professional sponsors it was always a challenge to make ends meet. Zeus got his first big break when he was invited to compete in a large regional competition after one of the original contestants injured himself close to the contest date. Zeus made the most of his opportunity and had his best showing yet. Although he did not win, he impressed enough people to secure his first professional sponsorship. He was beyond elated, his dream was finally starting to come true. His star was just starting to rise when tragedy struck. Within minutes of leaving the gym after a late-night workout, Zeus and a fellow bodybuilder were the victims of an armed robbery in the parking lot. The armed gunman shot them both, to this day Zeus still does not know why the robber needed to shoot them? An undercover police officer was leaving the gym and heard the shots. She interrupted the robbery and called for an ambulance. Unfortunately, the armed gunman escaped into the night. Zeus and his friend required surgery to repair some muscle damage and both needed physical therapy afterwards. While in rehab he spent a great deal of time thinking about his life and his future. Bodybuilding seemed trivial to him at this point in his life, he felt the need to spend his life doing something more purposeful. Zeus was glad to be alive and was filled with the need to do more with his life. He was able to meet and thank the brave officer who came to their rescue that night. After meeting with her he decided he wanted to help people by making the life-changing decision to join the police force. His parents were not happy with his decision and assumed he would change his mind and return to bodybuilding once he was out of rehab. They were wrong, Zeus successfully completed his rehab and joined the police academy. He found his calling in an unexpected way.

Zeus still works out but only to stay in shape. He is of retirement age but even at his age, he still towers over most people. Since retiring from competitive bodybuilding he has reduced his muscle mass to something more manageable. Zeus Chaplin may be older and weigh less these days but he is still an imposing figure. Today he looks more like a Police officer than a bodybuilder. He keeps his face clean-shaven and wears a short fade haircut. If he ever starts to go bald he has already decided he would shave it all off before visiting any of those hair replacement type companies. Detective Chaplin has enough years of service to be eligible for a police force retirement but has no interest in retiring. He has been working hard his whole life, he will probably work until he is physically unable to. Zeus is at the top of his game and does not show any signs of slowing down. He is also a realist and knows he cannot do this job forever. In the last year or two, he has allowed himself to consider retirement although he would never dare share that with any officers at work. Police work is not as fulfilling to him as it used to be, and he secretly fears he may be falling behind the times when it comes to crime-solving methods and technology. Plus, the office demographic has changed over the years. Where once he was in the majority, now he looks up and finds himself surrounded by co-workers young enough to be his children. He often asks himself where the time went, he did not feel the years as they flew past. Lately, Zeus has been wondering if he is holding other officers back from achieving the rank of Detective by not retiring? The last thing he wants is to be the guy that stayed around too long because people took pity on him.

CHAPTER 6

A stunned Tanya is now in Police custody, she is arrested and read her rights. Once restrained, Zeus Chaplin guides her off the front porch and out toward the squad car. He introduces himself and explains that they were called out for a burglary call. As soon as they are alone, Tanya begins to tell Zeus about how she is just visiting from out of town. She is at the house because this is where her friends live. She also shares with the Detective how an old lady in a robe came out of the house and attacked her with a cast iron skillet. As he is walking away she overhears Detective Chaplin ask one of the officers to take pictures and a sample of the blood on her hands. Up until that moment, she has not noticed the blood on her hands and forearm. Tanya looks on while the officer snaps pictures of her hands and swabs a sample. Once the officer is done she takes the opportunity to examine her hands and forearms for cuts. There are no injuries to her body that she can see, the blood on her hands must not be hers. She feels a sense of relief when she concludes it is not her blood, but that moment is quickly followed by a deep panic as she tries to think who's blood it could be? Tanya does not remember touching any blood. From the back of the squad car, she can see the silhouette of a body with a sheet draped over it get taken down the porch stairs on a gurney. Until that moment she had forgotten about the dead body, she had been so focused on what had happened to her. She feels the guilt now sitting in her stomach. Here she was battered, bruised, and disorientated but alive.

The concerned elderly house occupant nervously watches through the living room window and is desperate to come outside. Zeus Chaplin had ordered her back inside the house earlier and has noticed her anxiously observing through the front window. The elderly woman is clearly trying to follow what is happening outside while also trying to get a Police Officer's attention. Zeus is the lead officer on site, so he is responsible for the crime scene. He figures he should go and get a statement from the woman inside the house before she tries to come outside again. He would rather break the news of the death to her inside the home than out on the porch surrounded by Police tape and evidence markers. Zeus steps up onto the front porch and rings the doorbell. He looks over the scene where the body in the rocking chair was sitting. The chair is empty and hauntingly still now. There is an officer processing the scene. There is no response to the doorbell, perhaps it is not working? He opens the screen and politely knocks on the front door of the residence. Before he can finish knocking he is greeted at the door by an elderly woman. The woman is tall and stocky with jet black hair that she obviously dyes. She is dressed in a velour jogging suit. Zeus has not seen a velour jogging suit in years, but it looked comfortable.

"Good afternoon. I'm Detective Chaplin, may I come in and have a word with you?"

The elderly lady steps back from the doorway and allows the Detective to come inside. Zeus asks her for her name and if she is the homeowner. He reaches in his pocket for his notepad to write down the lady's answers. The elderly lady's name is Ms. Claudine Washington and she lives in the home with her cousin Sterling. Following her failed marriage, decades ago, she returned to using her maiden name of Washington. Once inside the two of them sit down in the living room and Zeus questions her about what she saw and heard. Ms. Claudine reveals she is the one who called the Police to report somebody breaking into her house. She states the person on the porch is her cousin, Sterling. She did not realize he was out there until she heard him yelling for help. Her thoughts turn to her cousin's condition. "How is my cousin?" asks a very concerned Ms. Washington. This is not the direction that Zeus wants to go at this early stage of the interview, but Ms. Claudine is persistent. She refuses to answer any more questions until the Detective updates her on the status of her cousin. Finally, Zeus must tell her that her cousin has died from multiple stab wounds, but they will know more once the investigation is complete. As Zeus feared, Ms. Claudine was not up for answering any more questions after hearing the news of her cousin's passing. He tries anyway and mentions to her how Tanya claims she was attacked by an elderly woman that came out of this house. Ms. Claudine immediately dismisses the claim as being ridiculous. She denies attacking anybody on the porch and points out that she is a senior citizen.

"I didn't even go out there, I was too scared of what might happen", she states.

"I thought it would be better if the Police handle it, so I called them."

The conversation is interrupted by an uninvited third person entering the room. Ms. Claudine runs toward her and they hug each other tightly before she explains who this is. The uninvited person is her daughter Tanisha who let herself in. She explains that she also called Tanisha after calling the police. "Are you here alone, where is the housekeeper?", wonders Tanisha. Ms. Claudine tells her the housekeeper left early. The daughter's arrival unofficially signals the end of the interview. Tanisha asks the Detective if they can ask her mother questions at another time because right now she needs to be with family. Zeus agrees and shows himself to the front door. Officer Chaplin feels concern over this type of crime happening here. This is not the typical call he has been getting in Viewgrove in past years.

Zeus is able to confirm the luggage at the scene belongs to Tanya and her ticket confirms she has just arrived in town by train. Although the railroad line is up and running, it is still a hot topic of debate around town. He is sure once word of this crime gets out that some of the older town residents will use this as a reason why the railroad line should not have been rebuilt. Zeus Chaplin is one of the people who voted for the railroad line to be restored. He felt it would be good for Viewgrove to be better connected to the surrounding cities. Tourism can also be a good source of funding for the local infrastructure. The Sunset Auditorium has led the way in attracting outside dollars by hosting various traveling productions like plays and even the now-famous Ms. Plus-No-Fuss Beauty Pageant. Just then Zeus had a thought. He reaches into his pocket and retrieves his flip phone. One of the young officers on the scene looks taken back at the sight of the phone. Zeus is used to and frankly tired of getting this type of reaction from young people.

"Haven't you ever seen a flip phone?", asks officer Chaplin.

"Only in old movies sir", carefully replies the young officer under his breath.

"I won't tell you how long I've had it, but it still works so why should I replace it?"

"I understand sir."

Zeus knew all too well that this young guy did not understand, he probably spends his money on the latest phone every year. Young officers are always complaining to each other about the cost of replacing their smartphone because they damaged theirs while in the line of duty. It is a conversation held around the Police Station all the time. He could buy at least two and a half phones for the cost of their one smartphone. As this retired psychologist he knows likes to say, "Youth is wasted on the young." Zeus scrolls through his directory and finds the number he is looking for. He presses send and listens as the phone dials.

CHAPTER 7

Myrtle has just set foot in her house and placed her purse down on the entryway table when her cell phone begins to buzz. She is returning from the Sunset Auditorium Committee's quarterly planning meeting. Myrtle loves serving on the Auditorium Board, but the meetings can run long whenever the votes are deadlocked. She threatened the other committee members with owing her both lunch and dinner if they kept her there any longer. Now back at home, whatever endorphins were gained from her morning walk have worn off and she is ready to plant herself on the couch. It feels good to be done with everything and back home. As soon as she walks through the front door she feels the day's stress fall away like heavy travel bags falling off her shoulders. The new health program she is on prevents her from passing through a fast food drive-through on the way home. Viewgrove does not have any drive-through vegan restaurants yet, so Myrtle will have to feed her hunger at home. For a split second, she remembers the phone ringer needs to be turned back on but then it is off to the kitchen and that thought is lost. Answering the phone is a low priority at this moment so she allows it to go to voicemail. This new healthy eating program still has her feeling a little grouchy, so she decides it is better to eat first to avoid taking it out on any callers. She checks her refrigerator to see if she has any more meal prep meals left.

Myrtle walks past the living room only to discover her cell phone is buzzing again. Ever since the case at the Sunset Auditorium she gets calls from numbers she does not know. They are mostly reporters looking for comment as they try to put a new spin on an old case she was involved in. Myrtle also hates telemarketer calls and she does not feel like listening to anybody's telemarketing pitch right now. She concedes and walks over to answer her cell phone which is over by the charger she had misplaced last night. The telephone number flashing on the caller display is familiar to her, this is far from a telemarketer, so she answers it. Myrtle is now in the habit of checking the caller ID before answering her cell phone and absolutely refuses to answer calls from blocked numbers. She picks up the call and instinctively places it on speaker.

"Hello, Detective."

"Hello, Myrtle?" answers Zeus Chaplin.

"How can I help you?"

"I'm glad I finally got you. Where have you been?"

Myrtle explains to Zeus how she left her cell phone on vibrate in the other room after she returned from the

Sunset Auditorium. She did not want it ringing during the meeting. Zeus, in turn, fusses at her for leaving her cell phone on silent. Despite his calling from a crime scene, Zeus still believes Viewgrove is a safe town. With that said he always reminds Myrtle to carry her cell phone with her, so she can always phone for help. Zeus Chaplin has grown rather fond of Myrtle, so he tends to be extra protective when it comes to her safety. He has never come straight out and told her how he feels about her, but she is a very perceptive lady, so he is sure she already knows. Myrtle has recently accepted a position as a Police Consultant which does require her to be somewhat accessible should her services be required. In her defense, a town like Viewgrove does not have enough cases to require her to be on-call full-time. Zeus cannot spend any more time fussing at Myrtle, although he would like to, so he gets to the nature of the call.

"I have some consulting work for you if you're interested."

He has a strong feeling she is interested, and it turns out he is right. Myrtle jumps at the opportunity to consult on a case. Zeus provides her the crime scene address and asks her to meet him at the house right away. Myrtle quickly locates a pen and scribbles down the address on the back of an electric bill envelope that happens to be sitting on the table. She hurries out to her car; the engine has not even had a chance to cool down from the drive home from the Sunset Auditorium.

Myrtle arrives at the crime scene in record time due to the limited traffic. Zeus is surprised how quickly she makes it and the cop in him assumes she was driving over the speed limit. "Good job on getting here so quickly." Myrtle is not in the mood for any jokes. The Detective was trying to pay her a compliment but that is not what she heard. She did not even acknowledge the Detective's comment. Myrtle had put her lunch back in the refrigerator and rushed to the scene. At the time she was too excited about consulting on a case to eat. Now she realizes what a mistake that was because the hanger (hunger-and-anger) is back. She is not herself when she is hungry. Zeus notices she is looking a little pale, but he has no idea why though.

"Are you feeling okay?"

"Yes, I'm fine", she quips.

The Detective was a little taken back by her response. He has worked with her in the past and they have never had an issue getting along. Myrtle cringes at the tone of her own voice, Zeus did not deserve that. She enjoys working with Zeus and is grateful he called her to assist. "I rushed out of the door before I could eat lunch", she explains to him. "I'm ready to work though, a broken crayon still colors." Zeus considers sending her home and not using her services on the case but then he has a better idea. "Oh, is that all?" laughs the Detective. He waves over one of the officers and orders him to purchase a healthy meal from a nearby diner and bring it back to the crime scene. Zeus keeps Myrtle company while the officer is gone by exchanging small talk and catching up. He is trying to distract her from the crime scene until the officer returns with lunch. It is no secret how quickly a crime scene can cause a loss of appetite. The Diner is a short drive away, so the officer returns promptly with a hot meal. She was unaware the Detective had even instructed the officer to make a food run. Myrtle is both surprised and touched by the gesture. Zeus lets her into the front passenger seat of his squad car where he knows nobody will bother her. Myrtle gladly eats her food and drinks her beverage in peace. The beverage happens to be one of her favorites too, strawberry lemonade with chunks of fresh strawberries in it. With each bite, she feels more and more like her old self. While on this healthy eating program she needs to pay attention to how often she eats to avoid another situation like today.

CHAPTER 8

Myrtle ducks under the yellow caution Police tape and officially steps onto the crime scene. She feels recharged and ready to work. Either she was extremely hungry or that was the best sandwich she has ever had. Either way, that sandwich was wolfed down in record time. It reminds her of her days as a school psychologist when she had to eat quickly at her desk because she was constantly being interrupted by students stopping by without appointments. Corned beef sandwiches are one of her favorites, but it is not something she would have ordered on this new meal program. Zeus had no way of knowing she was on a new diet program and in that moment, she was glad he did not. Myrtle is thankful for Zeus's kindness and makes a point to tell him as much. She feels a little guilty for not being a hundred percent ready to go when she arrived but plans on giving more than a hundred percent going forward. Myrtle makes her way over to Zeus to signal she is ready to begin work.

"So, what happened here, Detective?"

"Welcome back Ms. Jenson. How are you feeling?"

"Much better, I'm still adjusting to this new health program, no coffee this week."

Zeus invites Myrtle to walk with him while he briefs her on some of the main details. She asks if she can begin by taking a look at the victim first. They walk along the driveway toward the Coroner's hearse, so Myrtle may view the body. The hearse driver is preparing to leave and does not look pleased to see Zeus and Myrtle approaching in his side mirror. Although Myrtle is a local celebrity at the courthouse, she is not as popular at the coroner's office. She is officially a consultant for the VPD (Viewgrove Police Department), but some departments do not like to acknowledge her position and consider her nothing more than a common town citizen. The Coroner Department does not consider consultants as part of the law enforcement family and does not appreciate an outsider examining their work. There are more than a few town residents who believe Myrtle somehow skipped the line and a local resident should have the consulting position. Their belief is that Myrtle has not paid her dues and is receiving special treatment.

Zeus taps his knuckle rapidly against the back window of the hearse to get the driver's attention. The driver's head cocks slightly to the side, giving himself away, but he ignores the tapping. Zeus asks Myrtle to wait right there, he will be right back. The Detective walks around the hearse to the driver's side door and swings it open. The startled driver throws up both palms in a defensive position while leaning as far away from the open door as possible. "Do we have a problem here?" asks Zeus. The driver insists there is no problem and quickly asks how he can be of service. Zeus motions for the driver to unlock the rear swing door to allow them access to the body. The unnerved driver hurriedly fumbles with the automatic release button until he hears the click of the latch releasing. Had Zeus not been there the driver would probably have denied Myrtle access. The Detective does not have time to fully address the driver's attitude right then, but he makes a note to address it later. He makes his way back around to the rear of the hearse to find Myrtle staring at him. He knows why she is staring but he would rather not get into it right now. There are a few people with their opinions on Myrtle and that driver was just one of them. Zeus will deal with him later. He knows Myrtle runs on caffeine, sarcasm, and sassiness. She has given up coffee this week, so he is unsure how she will react to the driver's attitude. Myrtle stands 5 feet tall but when disrespected her attitude is over 6 feet. To try to avoid an incident, he makes up a story about the driver not being able to hear them because he was on the phone. A second reason for the lie is the professional embarrassment he feels over the driver's behavior. Nobody is fooled by the story and Zeus did expect that.

"Did he eat a bowl of frosted stupid flakes for breakfast?", asks Myrtle.

"He'll come around, or he'll have to find a new profession", answers Zeus.

Detective Chaplin has no tolerance for those who

mistreat people, it goes against the Viewgrove culture he has fought hard to cultivate. The hearse door lock clicks open, and Zeus rolls the victim's covered body out the back of the hearse to allow them easier access. The Detective retrieves a new pair of white latex gloves from his inside coat pocket and hands them to Myrtle to put on, "Be careful with these, it's the only pair I brought in a small." Dead bodies are something Myrtle never gets used to viewing. Even when she is serving jury duty the exhibit pictures of the victims are always difficult to look at. The white sheet covering the body is carefully lifted aside and the victim's body is revealed. "Who is he?" she asks. "His name is Sterling, Sterling Washington", replies Zeus. Myrtle leans over and whispers something into the victim's ear. The Detective cannot make out what she said, he is curious but decides now is not the time to ask. He watches as she examines the rest of the body. Sterling is an elderly man, possibly in his late seventies based on his skin and full grey five o'clock shadow that was starting to grow in. Interestingly he has a full head of jet-black hair that looks like it has been recently cut and obviously dyed. Myrtle believes this to be a sign of vanity or perhaps he is an actor or some other profession where it benefits him to appear younger. His fingernails appear to be professionally manicured. His hands have some blood on them which Myrtle assumes is his blood. She knows from serving on numerous jury panels, that blood can make blade handles slippery and hard to hold on to. So, it is possible some of this blood could be from his attacker. His attacker may have accidentally cut themselves while attempting to stab him. The medical examiner will be able to tell if it is all his blood. There are no other visible signs of the scuffle, his clothes do not appear to be torn or disheveled.

"You said this was a stabbing attack and not a suicide, right?" asks Myrtle.

The only sign of trauma to the body appears to be the multiple stab wounds, presumably from a knife blade or some other sharp object. She notices there are no cuts or visible puncture marks on either of his arms. Sterling's button up shirt and white undershirt are both punctured and soaked with his blood around the stomach wound. He is wearing a pair of khaki colored slacks and tan socks. On his feet, he has on what can be described as house shoes or slippers. Given how manicured Sterling's nails and hair are, Myrtle does not believe he would leave the premises in house shoes, this is a man that cared about his appearance. It is most likely he was attacked while sitting at home and very unlikely he was killed somewhere else and the body moved here. They will both know a lot more once the medical examiner has a chance to examine the body and complete a report. Myrtle likes to view the body just to get a sense for how it fits into the crime scene. Plus, seeing an actual body puts the police consulting work into perspective. There was a living person that was victimized, it is more than just reading evidence and profiling. This is somebody's brother, son, uncle, or father. She always insists on learning the victim's name for the same reason. Seeing a body and learning a name add a necessary level of humanity to something that can quickly become very clinical. Myrtle stretches the white sheet back over Sterling's body and closes the back door of the hearse.

CHAPTER 9

Zeus explains to Myrtle that he had a short talk with Ms. Claudine before she got there. Ms. Claudine informed him Sterling had lived in the home with her and that he was her first cousin. They had grown up together and bonded as they both had very little when they were younger. Very early on in their lives he became the brother she never had. The two cousins supported each other through good and bad times. Coincidently Ms. Claudine is watching everything happening outside through her living room window. Her attention turns to the new duo still walking around the crime scene while everybody else seems to be wrapping up and leaving. Ms. Claudine watches with great interest as the Police Detective trails a little brown skinned lady with short curly silver hair. Unbeknownst to Ms. Claudine, the silver curls are Myrtle's signature look. She wears her natural hair; however, Myrtle does own a few wigs for the occasional bad hair days. Her hairdresser tried to suggest lace front wigs to her as another option, but Myrtle prefers the natural look and wears very little makeup. The lace front wig does not make a lot of sense without makeup to conceal the lace. Myrtle is happy sticking with her regular slip on wigs, at night she can take them off and hang them up on the stands. Zeus follows close as Myrtle makes her way onto the porch. He is interested in watching her work, so he observes while keeping his distance, giving her space to operate. Zeus shares how he has ruled out suicide due to discovering Tanya at the scene with a scythe and blood on her hands. He says he is ninety-nine percent sure only because he cannot be one hundred percent sure until the coroner has finished her report. Myrtle moves through the police evidence markers on the porch to create a mental picture of what could have happened.

Ms. Jenson stands on the front porch and gazes out over the front of the property to get her bearings. She has gotten a little turned around while driving up the curvy driveway. It is a beautiful estate, complete with manicured green lawns bordered with mature golden weeping willow trees. The leaves from the trees are blowing gently in the wind. The main house is nestled behind a tree line. Some of the leaves have turned fall colors and fallen but enough remain to block any view of the front porch from the neighbors. The good news is the homeowners never have to worry about their privacy. The bad news is it is unlikely any neighbors saw anything due to the tree line. Myrtle feels there is a slim chance a neighbor heard anything, but it is still worth asking them. Detective Chaplin had the same idea earlier and had already dispatched an officer to talk to the neighbors before she arrived on the scene. The officer interviewed as many neighbors as she could find before returning to the crime scene with her findings. No surprise, the neighbors interviewed insist they did not see or hear anything out of the ordinary. Out there, without all the sounds of a busy town, any loud noises should carry a good distance. Myrtle begins to question if this was a random act or if it was planned? Did the killer choose to use a knife because they knew the sound of a gunshot would carry? The neighbors are not that close but surely a gunshot would attract unwanted attention and make it tougher for the killer to escape without detection. Then again, it is light outside, why would anybody plan this type of crime at this time of day? To commit such a crime in the daytime is so much riskier. Her next thought is, stabbing somebody to death with a knife is a very personal crime. Stabbing someone multiple times is usually a crime of passion, and not one committed simply for robbery. Detective Chaplin has informed her the young lady they found at the scene claims to be from out of town. A curious fact because this location feels a little remote, why would she travel all the way out here to commit her crime? There is no evidence that she drove herself here or had any way of getting back to where she came from. Where is her getaway car? Zeus states the young lady claims she took a taxi to the house. The Police state they did not pass any taxi on the way here. Is it possible the taxi was waiting for her and drove off once they saw the suspect stab the victim? The police have yet to confirm with the taxi company that a fare was driven out to the house earlier that day. While Myrtle is pondering the crime scene and trying to piece the evidence together, Detective Chaplin is busy working on his own theory.

Zeus believes the young lady in custody is very aware that this is the affluent part of town. This area has a reputation for being a safe, tight-knit community. It is not a big secret that a lot of the residents in this community are elderly and most are prone to leaving their doors and garages unlocked. Elderly is a term that Myrtle hates, Zeus makes a mental note to be careful not to use that term when explaining his theory to her. He believes the young lady, Tanya, somehow made her way out there to look for prescription drugs. Perhaps she hoped she would find an open door and raid a few medicine cabinets without the homeowners even knowing she was there. There is a better chance of the homeowners being away from the house during the daytime than there is at night. The suitcase she had with her is most likely part of her "lost tourist" act. She could also be a cat burglar, or she may just like breaking into homes and stealing random items for fun. Zeus believes this is a robbery attempt gone wrong. He is curious to examine the contents of the luggage she had with her to find out if it contains stolen merchandise? The Detective is also curious to speak to the mystery taxi driver. He wants to hear the driver's story, so he can ensure he is just a taxi driver and not a robbery accomplice.

Myrtle has completed her review of the crime scene. It looks like a rainstorm is fast approaching so her and Zeus decide to call the investigation off for the night. The medical examiner will not have any conclusive results until tomorrow, at the earliest. The two of them have just enough time to make it to their cars before the rain begins to pour.

CHAPTER 10

Early the next morning, the Medical Examiner (M.E.), Janna, clocks into the laboratory as she has done every day this week. "Coffee, she needs coffee before she can function correctly", she mutters to herself. Janna scuffles her way over to the makeshift kitchenette area set up in the laboratory. In the cupboard is the last of her special brew. The Medical Examiner's Office provides free coffee for employees, however, nobody in the building can stand to drink it. The coffee drinking employees usually bring their own coffee and serve that company crap to visitors. Janna is convinced the Department buys the cheapest coffee they can find. Fortunately, there is just enough of her personal stash to brew one last pot. Janna leaves the empty coffee bag on the counter to remind herself to bring in more special brew from home. The coffee pot starts to percolate and the aroma of coffee beans fills the immediate area. While waiting on the pot to brew she starts to prepare for the day. A glance at the work log reveals a body was brought in yesterday after hours. That body will have to wait, right now it is time to drink coffee out of her favorite mug with, "I See Dead People" printed on it. Her second favorite mug is her "Coffee is always a good Idea" mug. She took it home one night to wash it and keeps forgetting to bring it back to work. Janna clutches the hot cup with both hands as she raises it to her lips for that first magical sip. "Ahh." There is nothing like that first cup, she feels better already. It does not take her long to be done with that initial cup, her day can now begin. Janna pulls the work chart off the wall and everything is a lot clearer now that the coffee is running through her veins. She pulls on a pair of white latex gloves and prepares to examine Sterling's body. The Medical Examiner is finishing up her examination when she receives some uninvited visitors.

Janna can hear the footsteps echoing down the hallway. She is not expecting any company this early in the morning. The Examiner's Room is in the basement of the building and is not usually a place people like to visit. Most people stay clear of the Examiners Room to avoid accidentally seeing exposed body organs and losing their appetite. The double doors swing open and in walks Detective Zeus Chaplin along with Myrtle Jenson. Zeus greets Janna with a big smile and introduces Myrtle.

"Good morning Janna, this is Myrtle, she's a Police Consultant."

"Hey, Detective, what brings you down to the dungeon so early in the morning?"

"Can I offer you and your girlfriend a coffee?" asks Janna.

"Only if it's from your private stock and she's not my girlfriend."

Janna and Zeus share a laugh like old friends sharing an inside joke. Myrtle does not appreciate the "girlfriend" remark and does not even try to figure out the private stock reference. The Examiner's Room is a different work environment from what Myrtle is used to working in, she has not learned all the slang yet. She must assume either the coffee here is horrid, or it is code for adding liquor to their coffee. Unsure and not wanting to ask, she passes when offered a cup of this "private stock" coffee. Her mouth says, "No thank you", but her mind says, "Not today Satan." Zeus grabs the sleeve of foam cups from alongside the water dispenser and removes one from the plastic for her to pour coffee into. Janna takes slight offense to Myrtle declining the coffee, she just does not offer it to anybody. Some of the friendliness appears to leave her as she asks the reason the two of them are there. Nobody comes down to the dungeon unless he or she wants something. "So which body do you want to know about?" Zeus senses the change in attitude as well, he is disappointed because they were off to such a good start. He takes a sip of the coffee and compliments Janna on her homebrew before explaining that they are there about the body from yesterday. The Medical Examiner points at the body on the stainless-steel examination table. "You're in luck, I just finished that one." She goes on to list the contents of the stomach and other gory details Myrtle is not interested in learning. There was no skin or DNA recovered from under the victim's fingernails. There were no signs of puncture wounds on the hands, arms, or neck. The determined time of death is consistent with the crime scene. This is not a case of the victim being dead for several days before being discovered. The blood pooling pattern is also consistent with the victim being stabbed while seated in the chair. There is no sign the body was transported and placed there from a different location. The molds of the stab wound patterns match the blade of the bloody scythe that was recovered at the scene. The medical examiner can confidently conclude the body was stabbed several times with that blade of the scythe. There is still a small question of whether it could be an act of suicide? Myrtle asks Janna if she can be medically sure about the cause of death?

"Suicide is unlikely. Besides, don't we have a suspect in custody?", asks Janna.

"How did you hear about that?", asks Zeus.

"I work with dead people all day, but you'd be surprised what gossip I hear down here."

Finally, Myrtle is getting some information she is interested in. The Medical Examiner pauses her oral report long enough to flip the page on her clipboard. Myrtle uses the pause as an opportunity to ask another question. "Were you able to determine if there was more than one person's blood on the blade or on the victim's hands?" Janna's first thought is to remind Myrtle that this is not like one of those crime shows on television, things here take time. In a mild show of restraint, Janna curtly states the toxicology report is not back yet. If there were any drugs in his system, they will have to wait to find out. Janna is a good medical examiner, she just does not have a lot of daily interaction with live people so her social skills are not the best. Myrtle is unfazed by Janna's social skills and lack of tact. In her opinion, anybody whose job it is to cut people open and examine stomach contents or worse for a living is allowed a few quirks. Janna communicates to Zeus that, if he is interested, she can print out a copy of her preliminary notes for him to take with him. It goes without saying that this is completely off the record and a huge display of trust. Zeus knows the official report will not be ready for another few days. If it had not gone well, the medical examiner could possibly make them wait until the official post-mortem report is filed. He feels the trip to the Examiners Office is, therefore, a success. Myrtle, on the other hand, cannot get out of the Examiners Building fast enough. "Pardon the pun but I'm dying to get out of here", she whispers to Zeus on their way out. The Detective recognizes Myrtle does not yet know the different dances that come along with working with each department. She will need to learn the unofficial rules to survive in that ecosystem and receive maximum cooperation in the future.

CHAPTER 11

The walk back to the squad car is an unusually quiet one. Neither Zeus nor Myrtle speak as they get into the car. He can feel her eyes burrowing a hole in the side of his head, but he does not dare look at her. If he turns to face her she will see the huge grin on his face that he is trying to hide. Once the car doors close Myrtle is the first to break the silence. The only previous sound had been the chirp when the doors unlocked. She has been trying to let it go but she just must ask.

"So how was that special brew?"

Zeus lets out a loud belly laugh. He has been waiting for her to ask, he knew it was bothering her. Myrtle is not good at just letting things go. There was no doubt she was going to bring it up, it was just a matter of when. Once he has had his good laugh he explains that the Medical Examiner is a good example of why not to judge a book by its cover. Janna may be a little weird, but the coffee is actually pretty good.

"You should have seen the face you made when I took that first sip, it was priceless!"

Zeus thought the Medical Examiner was going to throw them out there and then. Janna takes her coffee brewing seriously, so Zeus is never worried about drinking any of it. Even with that said he admits that he always uses one of the company supplied cups in the plastic, just to be on the safe side. He cannot bring himself to drink out of any of those custom mugs sitting out, there are dead bodies down there after all. Not to mention what kind of dead body particles could be floating around in the air and landing in open mugs. Myrtle is getting creeped out just thinking about it and begs him to change the subject.

The traffic is light this time of day. Driving a squad car through traffic causes all the surrounding cars to immediately start obeying all the rules of the road. Myrtle is amused by all the cars slowing down once they notice the Police Car. The conversation in the car steers back toward the case and what they know about the victim. Myrtle and Zeus go back and forth about what they have learned so far and if any of it is relevant. She picks up the copy of the examiners preliminary notes that Zeus printed out before they left the building. She was secretly hoping he would print the report out from the Police Station because she was in a hurry to just get out of that Examiners Room. Myrtle eagerly flips through the pages of the report in hopes of learning more about the victim. The victim's name is Sterling Washington. He was seventy-one years old or seventy-one years young as Myrtle likes to think of it. Living to seventy-one meant he had already lived longer than the national average for men of color. However, he was robbed of the life he had remaining, he might have lived to see one hundred. He was 5 feet 11 inches tall with brown eyes and black hair. According to Sterling's most recent driver's license on record he lived at the address where he was killed. This matches what Ms. Claudine told Zeus during their short talk on the day of the murder. The Medical Examiner lists the stabbing as the cause of death but does make herself a side note to wait for the toxicology results before submitting her final report. There are some additional details about the blade wound dimension that Myrtle quickly brushes past. Gory medical details are just not her thing. She is however interested in another section of the notes. Janna's notes confirm Sterling's hair was dyed jet black. There is a side note referencing visible scalp damage. The M.E.'s best guess is some type of allergic reaction on the scalp and roots from the type of hair dye used, or possibly leaving the dye on the hair longer than recommended. This part bothered Myrtle for two reasons. The first being Sterling could have been dealing with great pain and discomfort. Why did his hairdresser keep dying his hair, was this just neglect on his or her part? She wonders if he was seeing a doctor for treatment. The second is he was a senior citizen and he could have been embarrassed and suffering in silence unnecessarily.

Myrtle points out to Zeus that there is no mention of Sterling Washington's palms being blood-soaked. She feels that as soon as he was stabbed he would have instinctively covered the wound with the palm of his hand. There should be blood all over his hands from him attempting to hold the wound closed, much more than what was present. So, he gets stabbed, but he does not make a lot of effort to stop the bleeding? His hands did not show signs of a struggle with an attacker. There is no skin from his attacker under his fingernails. There are also no self-defense cuts on his hands from the blade as he struggles to protect himself or attempts to pull the scythe away. To top off everything there are no usable fingerprints found on the scythe. Myrtle finds this highly suspicious and assumes the scythe handle and blade must have been wiped clean. With so many stab wounds there should be some prints from either the victim or his attacker. The Police determined the scythe was part of the homeowner's harvest porch display so there should at least be prints from the lady of the house. The Police theory is that the attacker, Tanya, used the scythe from the harvest display as a murder weapon. This all strikes Myrtle as odd because the crime scene exhibited signs of a major physical struggle. There were items knocked over and broken all over the porch, yet the Police report states the victim was found dead in the chair.

"This whole thing just doesn't pass the sniff test", blurts out Myrtle.

Her interest switches to where the victim was found. Did he sit down in the chair after the stabbing to rest? Zeus believes that is very possible. Myrtle points out there was no blood trail on the porch from somebody moving around or getting into an altercation. According to the Police, Tanya was the last person to see Sterling Washington alive. Myrtle wonders if she saw anything that could be helpful to both her and the investigation.

CHAPTER 12

The next destination is the Viewgrove Police interrogation room. Zeus invites Myrtle to continue to ride along to the next stop instead of going back for her vehicle. Ms. Jenson does not require a lot of convincing. Tanya was arrested at the scene so they are both interested in hearing what she has to say. They walk into the interrogation room where their interview subject is seated and waiting. "Good morning, my name is Detective Chaplin, and this is Ms. Jenson. Ms. Jenson is consulting with the Police and will be sitting in on this interview." Myrtle can read the fear on Tanya's face that she is trying to hide. She would hate to see this young lady spend time in jail if she is innocent. There are already too many people serving time for crimes they did not commit.

Zeus asks Tanya if she has any additional forms of identification? The State Identification card she is carrying in her purse is old, expired, and the picture does not quite look like her. The explanation he receives is that it is an old card and she has lost some weight and changed her hair since then. The Detective accepts that answer for now, but Myrtle can tell from his body language this is not the end of it. Zeus asks Tanya to describe, in her own words, what happened yesterday? She is glad to finally have a chance to tell her story, and believes it will clear up the whole situation. Her story begins when she arrives at the victim's home and walks up the steps to the porch. The reason she is there is to meet up with friends to collect donations for the local animal shelter. She says she collects donations for animal shelters every year, but this is the first year collecting with these friends. There is a man in a rocking chair on the porch, so she decides to ask him for a donation first. Tanya approaches him and touches the portion of his hand peeking from under the throw blanket to wake him up. The hand feels cool to the touch. As she reaches around his wrist to feel for a pulse, she is startled as a hand suddenly reaches up and grabs hers. In a weak raspy voice, he cries out.

"She's killing me, she's killing me!"

Tanya summons all her strength and with everything in her, she pulls her hand free from the cold clutch. The force from her pull causes her to knock a table and some chairs over as she collapses back onto the ground. This is no time to be defenseless, her brain is shouting at her body to get up. Tanya's voice is hoarse, her heart is racing, and she is breathing heavy. Only now does she realize she has been screaming the whole time. She pulls herself up off the ground while keeping an eye on the body in the rocking chair. This is not a movie, but she fully expects the person in the chair to stand up and attack her. The person in the rocking chair is not moving though. Tanya does not want to take any more chances, so she flattens herself against the house so she can keep as much space as possible between her and the rocking chair while she makes her way off the porch. She carefully inches past the person in the rocking chair. She is as far as the door and almost at the steps leading off the porch. She will feel much safer once she is down those steps and in the open space. The whole time she never takes her eyes off the person in the rocking chair. Just then Tanya receives the second biggest scare of her life as the front door to the house violently flings open with enough force to cause it to ricochet back off the wall. Out leaps an old lady wielding a cast iron pan wildly over her head and yelling.

"Who's out here screaming?!", she yells.

It took everything in Tanya's power to avoid getting struck in the face with one of those initial wild swings of the cast iron pan. She does not know how she managed to duck and avoid anything in her frenzied state of mind. Who is this crazy lady?

She will have to figure out who this lady is later, right now she needs to survive this new threat. The elderly lady swings again. This time Tanya throws her body on the porch to avoid getting hit. The old lady closes in on her to capitalize on her being vulnerable, lying face down on the porch. The best Tanya can do is turn over enough to face her attacker. She is unable to rise to her feet, all she can do is inch backward on her behind in a feeble attempt to put distance between her and the assailant. The old lady has the cast iron pan cocked above her head as she approaches. Now standing directly over her, she confronts the intruder about finding her on her porch.

"I said, who are you and what are you doing on my porch?!"

Tanya has run out of space and ways to hide, she is cornered. She comes to the grim realization that she is not going to be able to outmaneuver her attacker any further. She is trapped on this porch between the man in the rocking chair and the lady waiving a cast iron pan aggressively toward her. Tanya goes into survival mode, she needs answers and she needs them quickly. She just starts blurting out information as fast and as loud as she can. Her hope is that some of what she says makes sense to the lady threatening her. There is no way to be sure because she cannot make much sense of what is coming out of her own mouth. Trying to find better ways to explain herself is not going well. Her throat is sore, and her voice is hoarse. Her mouth and brain are just not working together. Tanya has resolved herself to the fact that she is most likely going to get smacked with that cast iron pan. She balls her body up as best she can to absorb the hits that are sure to follow. Her hands cover her face, leaving as little exposed as possible. The old lady does not appear moved by the rambling answers she is being given by this trespasser. Tanya takes a last look at her attacker through a small gap between the fingers she is using to protect her face. This is the last glimpse of her attacker she sees before she passes out.

Tanya slowly awakens to find herself lying on the porch floor. She struggles to keep her eyes open as they adjust and focus. How long has she been passed out? Through squinted eyes, she scans her surroundings. Her heart immediately jumps with the realization that she is still on the porch. The last thing she remembers is being cornered by the woman yielding the cast iron pan. Tanya turns her head from side to side frantically looking for the whereabouts of the old woman. Thankfully, there is no sign of the raging old woman who confronted her earlier. Her body is sore, and it hurts to move but she is determined to get out of there before any other crazy people arrive. How and why is she still here? She tries to speak but her throat is still raw, presumably from the screaming earlier. Not only is she still on the porch but she is back near the figure perched in the rocking chair. Unable to verbally communicate, Tanya calmly reaches out to touch this figure's hand to ask for help. The figure's hand is ice cold to the touch. She snatches her hand back as a reflex. The seated figure does not respond. She bravely reaches out to touch the figure's wrist. Once again nothing happens. It becomes painfully clear the man gently rocking in the chair is not sleeping, he is dead. Tanya swears to Zeus and Myrtle she would never kill anybody, and if that man is dead he must have committed suicide by stabbing himself. She admits to blacking out but feels the blood on her hands must have come from her trying to help him after he stabbed himself. "I don't remember anything that happened between being attacked and the Police arriving."

CHAPTER 13

The interrogation room looks just as Myrtle imagined it would. The interior walls are a sterile blue-grey color or at least that is how they appear under the artificial fluorescent lights. The walls are bare and there are no windows to let in any natural light. There is only one way in and out of the room. The furnishings consist of a table and three chairs, two on one side of the table and one on the other. There is no clock hanging on the wall in the interrogation room, so an interviewee does not know exactly how long he or she has been in there. Without the distraction of watching the clock, a person-of-interest has nothing to focus on but the questions and their reflection in the two-way mirror. A bonus for the Police is that the interview usually feels longer than it is. Suspects start to feel like they have been in there forever and get anxious to get out. The Police hope this will encourage suspects to tell the truth sooner, so they can chase down leads and close cases quicker. Myrtle is simply a spectator as Zeus conducts the interview, and is more interested in the interviewee's nonverbal cues. She estimates they have invested close to an hour into the process and it has been intense. Tanya is starting to show signs of fatigue, she is repeating herself and losing track of her spot in the story. Myrtle could use a break as well, she feels the walls closing in on her and she is not even the one being interviewed. Zeus seems to be the only one still going strong. He feels he may be close to a confession, so he keeps pressing Tanya about the details of the crime scene. Regardless of how hard Zeus presses her, she does not deviate from her story. Myrtle is expecting her to ask for a lawyer at any second but she does not. At one-point Myrtle is tempted to yell, "Objection!" herself. Zeus concedes for now and announces that they all need a break. "Finally!", screams Myrtle in her head. She is so glad to get out of that room she almost breaks into applause at the sight of the door opening to release them. Tanya is exhausted, but she will not let Zeus and Myrtle leave the interview room without stressing that she is innocent.

"Would you like a soda?" offers Myrtle.

"Do you mean a pop?" asks Tanya.

"Pop is a sound, I mean a soda."

"Coffee please", comes the answer.

Myrtle steps out of the room for a few minutes and returns with a cup of hot coffee. Tanya reaches out and accepts the coffee with thanks. The door closes again, and she is left alone in the interview room.

Tanya insists she is innocent so there must be other

suspects. Zeus is not ready to believe Tanya's story. "For all we know she could be an escaped mental patient who hallucinated the whole thing." Myrtle believes the evidence does point to other possible suspects. Based on all her years of psychologist training, she does not believe Tanya fits the profile of somebody who would commit this murder in this way. Not that she is not capable of murder, but Myrtle reads her as somebody more calculated. The circumstances of the murder feel very impulsive and the opposite of calculated. If Tanya is hiding something, it is not that she murdered Sterling in cold blood.

"What was her motive, money, jewelry, or drugs?"

Myrtle wonders if Sterling had his wallet and identification on him when he was found? Zeus, on the other hand, is not as convinced of her innocence. He has a few issues with her story. He cannot find a recent passport, driver's license or state identification for her. He is expanding his search, perhaps she will show up in a national database. Zeus searched the contents of Tanya's red suitcase earlier, and did find some jewelry. The only fingerprints on the recovered jewelry belonged to the homeowner, so Zeus assumes Tanya wore latex gloves. The problem is the Police did not find any gloves at the scene, they do not know where she disposed of them. Myrtle reminds Zeus of another problem which is the suspect was arrested with blood on her hands. Why would she use gloves to steal the jewelry but then take them off and risk getting blood on her hands when killing the victim? There was no blood found on any items inside the suitcase. Zeus figures the murder was unplanned and was committed after the robbery and after she disposed of the gloves. He makes himself a note to also check with the volunteer firemen to see if anybody recognizes her. Perhaps one of them can provide some useful information. Tanya has been allowed to use the phone and has placed a call on more than one occasion. No friends or family have shown up yet to the precinct to visit or bail her out, this makes Zeus wonder whom she is calling.

On the day of the murder, Zeus dispatched an officer to go around and interview all the neighbors. Myrtle now asks if she can review the officer's report. Zeus punches some information into his desktop computer and the report pulls up. He turns the monitor toward Myrtle allowing her to read the screen head-on. She puts on her readers and scans the report. A few minutes of silence pass before she speaks again. She points out that although the neighbors did not hear anything, a jogger did see a taxi cab leaving the long driveway around the time of the murder. The location of the property is in an affluent area of town and it is unusual to see a taxi cab. Residents in this area own cars and employ chauffeurs. It is not easy to access this area of town through public transportation either.

"We need to interview that taxi driver", states Myrtle.

Zeus is not all the way convinced this taxi driver exists. What if Tanya is creating this imaginary taxi driver to protect her accomplice? The same robbery accomplice that drove her out there and probably has the remainder of the objects they stole from other area homes. He explains to Myrtle that this taxi driver thing is a distraction to keep them busy. None the less, Myrtle insists on getting a description of the driver and cab from Tanya. Myrtle goes a step further and challenges Zeus, just to keep it interesting. She proposes that if they find the taxi driver, Zeus owes her an ice cream sundae of her choice from Anna's Diner. Now, if there turns out to be no taxi driver then she will march down to the medical examiner and get Zeus a whole bag of that homemade coffee that he was guzzling down.

Myrtle suggests they also track down some of Tanya's friends using social media, in case they have any idea what she is doing in town. The friends she claims she went to visit obviously do not live at Ms. Claudine's house, but do any of them live in the area? However, their online searches come up empty, they are unable to find any of her social media accounts. If there are any active social media accounts, they must not use her real name, or they have been deleted. Perhaps one of the other officers would have better luck, Myrtle and Zeus are not the most tech savvy. If they had been able to get into Tanya's phone they could possibly access her friends using her contact list. Unfortunately, Tanya's smartphone is locked, and she is refusing to unlock it. The phone maker is also refusing to unlock it. They may need to get a court ruling for permission to either hire a firm or order the phone maker to unlock the phone.

Zeus swivels his computer monitor back around and begins typing in another query, this time for registered taxi drivers. The look on his face says the list is a lot longer than he expected. There are a lot of names and addresses to sort through. Some of these people may not still be active drivers, the database only lists names of the people licenses were issued to. Myrtle can read the irritation growing on his face. She can tell he is frustrated with the search results. Zeus has been making a real effort to use his computer lately. In the past, he had purposely used it as little as possible and constantly had to reset more than one of his passwords whenever he eventually logged back on. Myrtle is impressed with his computer use today. She is constantly teasing him about his distaste for modern technology. At that moment, the initial pride she feels quickly turns to guilt for teasing him all of the time. Watching him makes it suddenly become real to her how different his life must be now that he is forced to learn all of this new technology for work. Zeus is a proud man and she knows he does not want to look foolish in front of his fellow officers for his lack of computer skills. She promises herself she will ease up on the jokes. After helplessly pecking away at the keyboard for a few minutes Zeus gives up.

"Come on, I think we'll have better luck on the street."

Myrtle and Zeus both agree to drive by the local hotels and train station. Taxi drivers often park at those locations in hopes of catching fares. Zeus can show Tanya's picture around to the drivers and see if anybody recognizes her. Perhaps they will get lucky and locate the alleged driver who dropped her off. Pounding the pavement is more of the Detective's style, he will take that over staring at a computer screen every day of the week.

CHAPTER 14

The Detective and the Consultant maneuver in the Police cruiser through the downtown streets on their quest to locate this taxi driver. Zeus knows all the quickest routes to get around the town. Myrtle does not come to this part of downtown often, it is amazing what you notice when you are not the driver. There are new businesses that were not there the last time she was in this area, which admittedly was a while ago. Most of the places Myrtle frequents now are within a small radius of her home. The sight of the changes made her wonder out loud what Viewgrove will look like in another twenty years. If this rate of growth continues the town will experience a lot of expansion. Town expansion is the exact opposite of the town's projected outlook several years ago. Quite a few years ago, the population was shrinking as young residents left in search of bigger opportunities. All this town history happened before Myrtle retired and moved to Viewgrove. No time for daydreaming though, right now there are more important things to focus on. The first place the

VPD cruiser pulls up in front of is the biggest hotel in town, The Capitol Hill Mansion. The Capital Hill Mansion is popular with business travelers due to its location in the Financial Ward. Taxis steadily park outside of this hotel in hopes of catching a business traveler's fare. The taxi cabs all line up in a row, if one gets a fare then the next car moves up to fill the vacant spot. There are three taxi cabs lined up and competing for fares at the moment. One driver prefers to stand outside of his car while the other two appear content to wait behind the wheel. The plan is to walk up to the line of parked taxi cabs and show them a picture of Tanya to see if any of them recognize her. From the looks of them, the taxi driver business attracts an assortment of different characters.

Zeus and Myrtle approach the first driver on what appears to be his smoke break. When shown the picture, the first taxi driver shakes his head and says he does not recognize her. This driver has worked as a taxi driver for over ten years. He is a veteran driver who drives every day as opposed to some part-time drivers who only drive during the tourist season. Car one's driver volunteers to check his passenger log anyway. As he opens his car door to retrieve his log, an old cigarette box falls out onto the ground. He confirms he has not driven a fare to that side of town in over three weeks. Myrtle and Zeus thank him for his cooperation before walking up to the next taxi. Myrtle is glad to be done with this driver and his cigarette smoke blowing in her face. He was trying to blow his smoke away from them, but the wind would carry it right back in her direction. Myrtle hates cigarette smoke, she feels it is a nasty habit. She was hoping Zeus would give him a ticket for littering. Tanya did not mention anything about smelling smoke in the taxi and this driver reeked of it. The second taxi driver has been watching them in her side view mirror. She rolls down her driver's side window as she sees the two approaching her car. Zeus identifies himself and explains why they are there. The taxi driver initially appears nervous but once she realizes it has nothing to do with her license she relaxes and is very cooperative. Driver two says she did not drive her cab yesterday because it was her day off. Myrtle takes a peek inside at the taxi's interior, it was not junky, but it looks like it has not been cleaned in a while. Zeus looks up toward the third parked taxi and locks eyes with the driver in the side view mirror. The moment Zeus makes a move toward the third taxi, the engine starts up, and it speeds off into traffic. Myrtle tries to get a look at the license plate, but the taxi accelerates into the distance too quickly. Zeus immediately turns back to the second taxi driver and asks who is driving the third cab? Unfortunately, the taxi driver does not know. She sees the cab a lot around town but does not know the driver's name. Myrtle flags down the first taxi driver and asks if he knows the identity of the third cab driver?

"Oh, that's Bibby, is he in some kind of trouble?"

"Is Bibby his real name? Do you know where we can find him?" asks Myrtle.

"I think his real name is Henry, I can't be sure, I know he likes to work the train station."

Before Myrtle has finished talking to the driver, Zeus has pulled the Police cruiser up next to her and is yelling for her to jump in. She quickly obliges, and off they go in pursuit of the taxi. The trail goes cold and Zeus is upset with himself for losing sight of the cab. "All is not lost", offers Myrtle, "I learned he usually works fares from the train station." They both decide to see if he makes an appearance at the train station today. Zeus checks his watch, the next train is not due to arrive for at least another hour.

An hour later Myrtle and Zeus are staking out the train station, closely eyeing every taxi that pulls up. To avoid detection, they arrived at the station way ahead of the scheduled train time. Myrtle uses the extra time to show Tanya's picture to the taxi drivers parked outside of the station. Not one of the drivers recognize Tanya but they all know Bibby and can supply a description of him. Just as the train is pulling into the station, a new taxi cab arrives. The cab does not stop and line up in the taxi zone right away, instead, it circles the station a few times before eventually parking in the taxi loading zone. Myrtle watches this cab circle around and thinks to herself, "This has to be Bibby." She figures he must be checking to see if the coast is clear before he parks. Myrtle anticipated Bibby being cautious about returning to the train station. She was not sure if he would be smart enough to stay away but she is glad that he was not. Zeus has hidden the Police cruiser out of sight just in case Bibby shows up. He too watched as the taxi arrived and circled the station a few times before parking. Myrtle quickly wraps the scarf she just purchased in the station gift shop around her head, and puts on a pair of sunglasses before going out to try to get into Bibby's taxi. The other drivers call out to her as she walks past them and chooses the taxi she wants. Bibby is grateful to be chosen ahead of his fellow taxi drivers that have been waiting longer. He extends a warm greeting to his passenger and asks if she has any luggage? Once he confirms there is no luggage to load he slams the trunk of the taxi closed. Bibby moves around from the trunk and opens the back door for Myrtle. Upon securing the door closed he happily runs around the front of the car and hops in the driver's seat.

"Where to ma'am?"

"The Sunset Auditorium please", replies Myrtle.

Bibby shifts the car into drive and they pull away from the curve and merge into traffic.

Everything about this cab ride feels perfectly normal. Bibby asks if she would like him to turn the radio on to either music or the news? Myrtle politely declines the offer and then wonders if she should have accepted it. Did her answer make her sound nervous? Who chooses to ride in silence? He is going to know something is up. She has no experience being undercover and it is the two of them alone in a moving vehicle. In her mind she knows Zeus will be following them, but she is still a little on edge. Bibby appears unphased by her declining the offer to turn on the radio. He is quite content to hum to himself as they travel down the road. In any event, Myrtle keeps a hand on the door handle in case she is forced to roll out of the car onto the street. Now, she has only seen this maneuver accomplished in action movies and seriously doubts she has the courage to actually jump out.

CHAPTER 15

To Myrtle's relief Bibby does not appear to recognize her, she pulled this makeshift disguise together in a hurry once she spotted his taxi arrive. There was no guarantee Bibby would even show up. Part of her is not surprised he does not recognize her seeing as he was probably too focused on Zeus. Anybody would be focused on a large Police officer approaching them, it is quite understandable. Myrtle examines the interior of the taxi and finds it to be immaculate. Either Bibby is a neat freak, or he has just had this interior cleaned. Bibby's cab does not get more than five miles away before he notices the flashing Police lights in his rear view mirror. He turns down a different street and changes lanes in hopes the lights are not for him, and the Police car will go past him. Unfortunately for Bibby, those lights are for him. As soon as he changes lanes, the Police car pulls right behind him. For a split-second, Bibby has an impulse to try and outrun the Police but he quickly comes to his senses for two main reasons. The first reason being he has a passenger and does not want to be charged with kidnapping. The second reason is Viewgrove is a smaller town so eventually, he would be caught. Bibby slows down and pulls over to the side of the road. The Police car pulls over behind him with the lights still flashing. The officer emerges from the squad car and to Bibby's dismay, it is the same one from outside the hotel earlier. Detective Zeus Chaplin's imposing figure makes it very easy to remember him. Bibby rolls down his driver's side window and gets his registration and license ready. Zeus reaches the taxi cab window and flashes his badge. "I'm Detective Chaplin and your passenger is Ms. Jenson, she's a Police consultant." Myrtle notices the fresh cuts on Bibby's hand as he passes the Detective his license and registration through the window. Zeus examines the documents to confirm they have the right person, then wastes no time with pleasantries. He presents the picture of Tanya and asks Bibby if he recognizes her.

"No, she doesn't look familiar", replies Bibby.

When Bibby asks what this is about, Zeus questions him about his whereabouts the day before. The taxi driver gives a casual answer about taking fares around town but does not give many details on the destinations. When questioned again about his whereabouts the day before, he vehemently denies being anywhere near that part of town. He insists he declines fares looking to travel to that side of town. Bibby's body language feels off to Myrtle. She reads his lack of eye contact, touching of his neck, and rubbing of his nose as deceptive so she plays a hunch.

"Bibby, what do you have to say about this earring I found nestled in the back seat?"

"What earring?", protests Bibby, "Nestled, who even talks like that?"

"This matches our suspect's missing earring, I wonder how it got in your taxi?"

Myrtle holds up a single gold earring as she describes to Bibby how the earring makes him a person of interest in a murder investigation. Bibby does not turn around to properly look at the earring but instead glances at it sporadically in the rear-view mirror. Myrtle can tell that he is rattled but he sticks to his story and continues to assert he does not recognize the lady in the picture. Myrtle points out that the Detective could impound his taxi for days or weeks while the investigation is ongoing. Picking up on Myrtle's cues, Zeus assures Bibby he can have a tow truck there in ten minutes to impound the cab and he can catch a ride back to the station with them in the back of the squad car.

"Okay, okay, please, no need for any of that to happen", pleads Bibby.

Presented with these new circumstances, Bibby makes a business decision and admits to lying to them. "I'm sorry I lied to you earlier." He admits he did pick up Tanya from the train station and take her to the residence that day but insists that is all he did. Bibby claims he lied because he did not want to be involved in whatever Police matter she is involved in. He had a lot of run-ins with the law as a juvenile and still lives with a distrust for law enforcement. Zeus circles back to the question of Bibby's whereabouts? The taxi driver swears he spent the time driving around looking for his next fare. "How did you hurt your hand?"

asks Myrtle. Bibby looks down at his hand as if he is unaware it is even injured. "Oh, I forgot those were there, I cut myself working on an engine three days ago", he answers. Myrtle opens the taxi door to let herself out. As she is exiting she glances over at the fare meter then reaches back into the cab and pays what the meter says is owed. "What, no tip?", asks Bibby in a nervous attempt to determine if the situation is de-escalated. "Here's a tip, don't leave town", replies Myrtle as she pushes the back door shut.

As soon as Bibby hears the back door close he slowly pulls back into traffic and pulls away at a reasonable speed. Zeus explains to Myrtle that Bibby is free to go for now, but he may be called upon later. After interviewing the taxi driver, Zeus must admit that Tanya could have been telling the truth. He does not want to go as far as to believe she is innocent, but he cannot deny she told the truth about the taxi cab. Once back in the squad car Zeus reminds Myrtle the earring she found is evidence, and needs to be added to the evidence log as soon as they get back to the station.

"Oh, no need for that Detective, it's my earring."

"I wish you wouldn't do stuff like that", lectures Detective Chaplin.

Myrtle explains how she felt Bibby was protesting way too much, so she played a hunch. It is not the first time a little psychological subversion has helped her get to the bottom of a situation. Zeus cannot deny the results, but he warns Myrtle to run things by him first before she tries anything like that again. The squad car merges back into traffic and they travel to their next destination in silence. Myrtle is the first to break the silence by reminding Zeus that she won the bet and she intends to collect. He had forgotten all about their wager. There was indeed a taxi driver and they found him, so the Detective owes her an ice cream sundae from Anna's Diner. He does not really mind that he lost, and he always makes good on his bets. Had he won and got the homemade coffee he would have brewed and drank the whole bag just on principle.

Zeus points the squad car in the direction of the Police station. Myrtle presumes he is headed to either update the case file or perhaps work some of his other open cases. It is hard to tell from his body language if he is still irritated about the earring stunt. He appears unfazed by the taxi driver discovery moments ago. Whereas, Myrtle is still riding high on an adrenaline rush, she feels energized. After the success of the taxi driver interview, she is not ready to just go back to the station. Her thought is they should continue with the case while the trail still feels hot. How can she make Zeus see it her way? Truthfully the only thing waiting for Zeus at the Police station is paperwork and more paperwork. Myrtle does her best to remind him of this fact. To her surprise, he is easier to convince than she thought. Her feeling is that if there were a serious matter or a radio call came in she would have been unsuccessful in persuading him. Myrtle suggests they take a detour and pay the victim's cousin, Ms. Claudine, another visit. They were planning to have another talk with her tomorrow anyway. Zeus agrees and changes course toward Ms. Claudine's residence. He is stubborn and only does want he really wants to do. Myrtle knows if he goes along with any suggestions it is because he wants to and not for any other reason.

CHAPTER 16

Myrtle discusses the case with Zeus during the drive. The time passes quickly and before she knows it they arrive at Ms. Claudine's home. Zeus is the first up the porch steps to ring the doorbell. Ms. Claudine answers the door looking very surprised to see them.

"Good afternoon ma'am, my name is Detective Chaplin, we spoke yesterday. Ms. Jenson is consulting with the police. We came to finish getting your statement."

"I'm in my bathrobe, I thought you were coming tomorrow?" questions Ms. Claudine.

"Yes, but we were in the neighborhood, so we stopped by."

Ms. Claudine is accustomed to expensive things and it shows even in her taste in robes. Myrtle is too busy admiring the five-star luxury hotel quality robe to hear much of what the Detective said. A bathrobe is too common a name for this royal garment, this is no mere bathrobe. Myrtle's mind reminisces about the luxurious robes from a first-class spa retreat she once experienced years ago. They were these large organic cotton robes with monograms engraved on the upper left-side panel. She is so tempted to ask where she can purchase a robe like this, and hopes she can work it into the conversation later? Ms. Claudine steps to the side and opens the door wide enough to allow Zeus and Myrtle entry to her home. She guides her uninvited guests into the parlor room right off the front door foyer before excusing herself to change clothes.

Zeus rises to his feet when Ms. Claudine re-enters the room. "Please Detective, sit down, make yourself comfortable." Once seated again Zeus asks their host what she remembers from the day before? Ms. Claudine tells them how she had come back into the house from being outside. She had gone out in the morning to work in the garden before it became too hot outside. Whenever she works outside she always leaves the back door open, she does not want to risk locking herself out. "How embarrassing would that be?" Besides, the neighborhood she lives in is continually ranked the safest in town, so it is common for residents to leave their doors unlocked. Ms. Claudine pauses her story, and eyes her interviewers to gauge their interest. Zeus asks her to describe what happens next. The story picks up again with her washing the garden dirt from her hands in the kitchen sink. The curtains are still drawn over the parlor room windows. She enters the parlor room to draw back the curtains and let some sunlight in. That is when she notices Sterling sitting out on the porch in the rocking chair. This explains why he did not answer when she paged his room to come down for coffee. She fills her cup and is heading out to join him when she sees another individual on the porch. There is a young woman out there talking to Sterling. "Did you recognize the young lady?" asks Myrtle. "No, I did not, I've never seen her before." She admits she was being nosy and just watched from the window for a minute although she could not hear what they were saying. The two of them appeared to be having a regular conversation until suddenly, to her disbelief the young lady picked up the nearby scythe decoration and began stabbing an unsuspecting Sterling. Ms. Claudine is getting emotional while retelling the story. "I covered my mouth to muffle my screams. Sterling never had a chance, it happened so quickly he did not even get up from the chair. It is debatable if he even saw the blade coming." Although the scythe was part of the decorative displace it still has a real blade attached to it. Ms. Claudine confesses she is frozen with terror as Sterling sits there slightly slumped over. She can remember thinking, "This is a bad dream." Her eyes cannot be seeing what they are seeing. She is terrified for her own life, she tries to be quiet, so the young killer will not hear her and come after her inside the house. Ms. Claudine creeps toward the phone as quietly as possible and calls 911. The whole time on the phone she is trying to keep an eye on where the killer is and avoid being seen through the window. While she is on the phone with the operator she sneaks around to lock all the doors and prays there is nobody else already in the house. After she gets off the phone with the Police she calls her daughter. "Is there any footage available from the security cameras?", asks Myrtle. Ms. Claudine scoffs at the idea of security cameras. She is offended this Police Consultant would think she needs security cameras. "Viewgrove is a safe town, unlike whatever crime infested city you moved here from."

Ms. Claudine continues on to describe how she hid in the kitchen until she heard the Police arrive. "The young lady you arrested is definitely Sterling's killer", I hope she gets the harshest punishment allowed. Myrtle asks if the young lady, Tanya, tried to enter the house or if they had any interaction? "Weren't you listening?", exclaims Ms. Claudine. She turns to Zeus and asks him to tell Myrtle that she hid until the Police arrived. Ms. Claudine believes Tanya cased her house while she was out working in the garden. The door is open, so she could have easily come in and committed the robbery. Ms. Claudine's theory is the killer is robbing the house and hears her coming in from the back garden, so she tries to escape with the stolen goods through the front door. Maybe Sterling confronts her and that is why he gets stabbed. She has always tried to warn Sterling about trying to help everybody. "I tried to warn him about helping these deviants. This time it got him killed."

Ms. Claudine admits that in all the commotion she had spent the remainder of the day downstairs with friends and family in mourning. She mentions to Detective Chaplin that she needs to file a police report because she has jewelry missing and nobody was in her house but her and the murderer. She did not notice anything missing until after the Police had left and she went back into her bedroom. That is when she discovered some jewelry was missing. Zeus asks her to describe the missing jewelry. He shows her pictures of the jewelry found in Tanya's luggage and Ms. Claudine immediately identifies them as hers.

Ms. Claudine's house phone rings while Myrtle and Zeus are conducting their interview. She excuses herself to answer it but returns almost immediately to rejoin Myrtle and Zeus.

"It was a wrong number", she offers.

Myrtle asks permission to use the powder room. Ms. Claudine points her down a nearby hallway. Myrtle excuses herself and leaves Zeus behind to finish the interview. He asks if she and her cousin Sterling were close? Ms. Claudine assures him they were very close, and she cannot think of anybody who would want to hurt him. The Detective asks a few more questions before they are interrupted by the phone ringing again. Myrtle is prepared to rejoin the interview when she hears the house phone ringing. She slumps back into the hallway and out of view while she eavesdrops on Ms. Claudine's conversation.

"I told you to stop calling, I'll reach out to you when it's appropriate!"

With that, Ms. Claudine abruptly ends the call and walks back to where Zeus is seated. Once Ms. Claudine is safely out of view, Myrtle comes out to rejoin the two of them, but not before quietly picking up the receiver and checking the caller ID. She is shocked by what she sees.

Myrtle rejoins Zeus just as he prepares to wrap up the interview. He asks if she has any final questions for their host. Myrtle asks Ms. Claudine if her phone number is listed? She does not see where this line of questioning is going but she answers anyway just to get them out of her house. Ms. Claudine informs Myrtle she has no idea if her phone number is listed but assumes it is since she has not changed her home phone number in over twenty years. Her memory is not the greatest, but she does recall having the number transferred when she purchased the house. The new suburban home was purchased after the big train crash, that is why she remembers. Myrtle discovered soon after she arrived in Viewgrove that the residents use the big train crash as a time marker. It is common for local residents to divide their lives into two eras, there is before the train crash, and after the train crash. Myrtle asks if Sterling had ever complained of any pain, like head pain for example? The look on Ms. Claudine's face says she thinks it is a silly question. "Obviously he complained of pain, he was an old man", she snaps. Ms. Claudine gathers her composure before answering again, "No more than the usual aches and pains that come with being old, I'm sure you know how that is", she answers. Myrtle never misses a chance to snap back, "I have no idea, when I get your age I'll let you know." This leaves Ms. Claudine steaming because she swears Myrtle is as old as she is if not older. Zeus quickly thanks Ms. Claudine again for her time and hurries Myrtle out of there.

Once back in the comfort of the police cruiser Myrtle has a confession for Zeus. She really did not need to use the restroom, she just needed an excuse to look around a bit. Zeus warns her again, "That's strike two today." She admits she did not even find anything out of the usual to help the case. However, she did learn something about the phone call Ms. Claudine received. Myrtle held a beat, just for effect, before revealing what she has learned. The incoming call to Ms. Claudine was placed from the Viewgrove Police Station.

CHAPTER 17

Zeus screeches the car into an illegal U-turn in the middle of the street and heads in the direction of the Police Station. Myrtle braces herself against the dashboard and the door as she is unexpectedly tossed around the cabin. Wherever they were headed before Myrtle's revelation can now wait. Zeus asks three different ways if she is certain of what she saw, and each time Myrtle says yes. The ride back to the other side of town feels quicker, it is strange how the trip back to familiar territory always feel shorter. A motivated driver going over the posted speed limit also helps to reduce the travel time. Myrtle has not spent any time in Ms. Claudine's neighborhood, she has always thought it was too far out to frequent. She must admit to herself that the present company helps to make the drive feel shorter also. Myrtle is glad to be paired with Zeus on this case. If she had to work with any other officer on the force it may not go as smoothly. Zeus upholds the law, but he also allows Myrtle the freedom to work the cases in her own way. This is the main reason she accepted the consultant job. She was unsure when he originally asked her to become a Police Consultant, but she has enjoyed every minute of it. Myrtle views Zeus in a new light. Surprisingly she finds herself looking forward to collecting on their ice cream sundae bet.

Zeus parks the Police cruiser in the side lot and hustles into the station. Myrtle follows him inside but has to quick step to try to keep up with him. He heads straight for the Phone Desk. On his way, he gets paged by the Police Chief who is looking for an update on the case. He mouths to Myrtle that he will be right back, so apparently, he does not believe this will be a long call. Zeus motions for Myrtle to keep going. She knows where he was headed and exactly what he is looking for. Surprisingly there is no line at the Phone Desk. She gets the attention of the Officer on duty and requests the telephone logs. In the back of her mind she half expects to get some resistance from the Officer but to her surprise, he complies without any issue. Did he see her walk in with Zeus, or has word finally gotten around that she is a Police Consultant? It is not long before the search produces results. A lot of the calls can easily be eliminated leaving only a handful to sort through. Had the call logs been checked days later it would have taken a lot longer to sort through due to the additional entries. The Viewgrove Police Department's policy is to log all calls that suspects make from the station telephones. As soon as he concludes his call Zeus rejoins Myrtle at the Phone Desk. Myrtle is cross-checking today's numbers against the day before and sure enough, there is a match.

Myrtle and Zeus both agree they need to have another interview. The suspect is retrieved from her cell and led into the interrogation room to wait. The Detective and the Consultant walk in minutes later. "I'm Detective Chaplin and you remember Ms. Jenson." Tanya is surprised to be speaking with the two of them again so soon. Myrtle had not paid much attention to the suspect's physical characteristics the last time. During that interview, she was far more interested in collecting information. This new healthy living program really has her off her game. Today she takes full notice of Tanya as a person. The young lady has clear brown skin, a physique that says she works out, and naturally curly hair. She does not look a day over thirty although she is thirty-four years old. Zeus gets right down to business, "You called the victim's home both today and yesterday. What is it that you keep calling there about?" Tanya denies the accusation, "I dialed a wrong number. I was trying to remember a friend's number, but I misdialed it." The Detective keeps asking and she continues to deny it until he informs her they have reviewed the call logs. Myrtle tries to convince the young lady to make it easy on herself and admit the truth. "We're going to find out anyway, it's better for you if you tell us now." Tanya buries her face in her palms before finally admitting that they are right. "Okay, I'll tell you. I did make the calls." Zeus wants to know why she is calling the victim's family? It feels to him like a pressure tactic to get a reduced sentence or possible dismissal. The calls could be attempts to scare the victim's family from testifying. "It's not what you're thinking Detective, Claudine is my aunt."

Zeus and Myrtle are both shocked by the revelation. The shock is displayed all over their faces even though they are currently speechless. Complete silence takes over the room. Tanya feels like they do not believe her. She searches their faces for any sign of support or acknowledgment but finds none. The first thought for the Detective is not to believe her. The discovery of the taxi driver had him open to considering her innocence but that last comment wipes all of that away. He is back to believing wholeheartedly she committed the murder. Myrtle is just as surprised but is more willing to consider what they are hearing may be the truth.

"What did you say young lady?" asks Myrtle as if she did not trust her hearing.

Ms. Jenson heard exactly what was said but just needs to hear it again. Tanya repeats her previous statement and once again it is met with silence. She makes no attempt to keep the frustration of not being believed from showing on her face. It goes without saying that a revelation like this needs to be explained. The explanation given is that she is Ms. Claudine's niece and her being in town is the result of an unresolved family drama. According to her, Ms. Claudine and Sterling robbed her of a monetary settlement. She lived in Viewgrove years ago. Tanya's parents got divorced when she was twelve and her mother moved away. She grew up living with her father in town. When she was in the eleventh grade her father was diagnosed with cancer. He fought hard but lost his battle with cancer weeks after she graduated from high school. After the funeral, it was too hard to live in the family home anymore. Her aunt, Ms. Claudine, agreed to sell the house for her. After the funeral expenses were paid, she used the remainder of the life insurance payout to start a new life.

The first thing she bought was a train ticket out of town.

"Is this the first time you've been back to Viewgrove?", asks Zeus.

"Yes, it is, I haven't been back here since that day."

The psychologist in Myrtle makes her curious about Tanya's mindset. She left town all those years ago and has not been back until yesterday, was there a connection?

"What made you leave Viewgrove all those years ago?"

Myrtle's mannerisms remind Tanya of her grandmother. There is something nurturing about the way she asks, so she explains how everything had gotten so hectic once her father died. People act strangely after somebody dies, it brings out the best in some but the worst in most. Tanya felt like everybody was pulling her in different directions, everyone seemed to want something. In a matter of days, it had become all about money and material things. The same people who hugged her at the funeral and asked how she was doing were now calling to see what she was going to do with the house and its contents. The most common conversation now was if she wants to give away anything they would be more than willing to come to pick it up. Tanya was amazed by how people had such a detailed inventory of what was in the house. She was young and overwhelmed.

"I hate confrontations, I hate bickering over stuff, and so I left."

After several years of trying, a friend finally convinced her to seek out her inheritance and claim what is rightfully hers. The real reason she is back in town is to collect her inheritance. The reason she went to Ms. Claudine's house is to talk to her and Uncle Sterling about it. The last thing Tanya says before going back to her cell is that she came back to work out an agreement but swears she knows nothing about the murder.

CHAPTER 18

Ms. Jenson takes a walk down the hall toward the vending machines, not to get a snack, but to think. If she was a smoker she may have stepped outside to light one up. She just needs a moment to let what she just learned in the interview room settle in her mind. Out of habit, she eyes the selections in the vending machine but there is not one healthy option among them. This is not the time to fall off the wagon, she is still on this healthy eating program after all. The truth is the Police have a pretty good substantial case. Myrtle's focus is catching the killer whether it is Tanya or not, but she knows the Police need solid reasons to keep investigations open. There is a real chance that she could get convicted of this crime whether she is guilty or not. Withholding information only makes the investigation more difficult. Myrtle returns from the vending machines to find Zeus at the evidence board where he has been waiting for her to arrive. He is standing there calmly although the look when his eyes meet hers says, can you believe that? They have not talked about what they heard in the interview. They may never discuss what just happened, but Myrtle has a strong suspicion about how he feels. Zeus does not believe this new story about being Ms. Claudine's niece. Why would Ms. Claudine not mention this when they went over there? Why would she leave her niece in custody without attempting to post her bail? Ms. Claudine is wealthy, so it cannot be a financial issue. Why did Tanya neglect to provide this information when she was arrested? Yet again he thinks she did it, and is now doing whatever she can to throw off the investigation. Myrtle's suspicion is confirmed when Zeus turns to her for perspective on the matter.

"If you have a good theory why she didn't do it, I'd love to hear it."

Even Myrtle must admit that Tanya's story has some holes in it, although if that was her aunt it would make sense why she would be calling her house. Would she really go over to where Sterling lived and kill her uncle? None of this makes a lot of sense. There are no fancy animation computer programs or 60-inch monitors available on this case, Zeus prefers the old school whiteboard. Myrtle walks over to the whiteboard and with Zeus's permission updates the suspects' board to reflect as she sees things. She rearranges the headshots as she recaps what they know so far.

At the top of the board is the victim, Sterling Washington. Sterling lives with his cousin Ms. Claudine on the family estate in the affluent part of town. He has been retired from working for several years. Sterling was stabbed on his front porch. There were no defensive wounds. Sterling had minimal blood on his hands unlike they would expect to see when somebody is trying to stop a wound from bleeding out. There are signs of damage to his scalp. He does not appear to have any enemies. The lab was not able to get any clean prints from the scythe. The scythe handle appears to have been wiped clean. Was this truly just a random act of violence? Was there any family drama? He was married once but his wife died shortly after the wedding. They never had any children and he never remarried. Does anybody stand to gain from his death? Sterling does not have any adopted children. The family owns a few businesses which are mostly run by Ms. Claudine's children. Myrtle feels this is not an easy open and shut case, so they need to uncover if Sterling had a substantial life insurance policy or last will. Is there any way he could have done this to himself, even by accident?

Right under Sterling's headshot is a picture of Tanya. She appears to be from out of town, just arriving here yesterday. Is her first act in town to commit a murder? There was blood on her hands, what turned out to be Sterling's blood. However, there is no blood on any of the stolen items found in her suitcase. If she used gloves she did not stash them in the luggage. Did she stash the gloves somewhere in the house? There were no drugs found in the suitcase. Was the suitcase part of her plan to pose as a lost traveler to gain access to the home? Perhaps the suitcase was to transport stolen goods in? Did Sterling interrupt the robbery and she killed him to keep him quiet? She has no alibi for the time of the murder and cannot explain why she was found on the victim's porch. Tanya claims she blacked out after her aunt attacked her, and is being framed for a crime she did not commit. What did she use to wipe the fingerprints from the scythe? She did tell the truth about there being a taxi driver. Her claim is she is Sterling's niece and she is in town to collect on an inheritance she was robbed of years ago. It has been uncovered that she was making telephone calls to Ms. Claudine. Did she just look the phone number up in the phone book or does she remember it from childhood? According to the phone company records Ms. Claudine has not changed her phone number in over twenty years. Does Tanya have anything to gain from Sterling's death?

The third headshot on the board is the taxi driver, Bibby. Bibby drove Tanya out to the scene of the crime. He does not have a solid alibi for the time of the murder. Bibby appears to want to avoid any contact with law enforcement. Is there something in his past that relates to this case? Bibby also initially lied about having any contact with Tanya and attempted to avoid being interviewed. Myrtle has already checked, and Bibby does not have a criminal record, only a few minor traffic violations. Could he be a secret accomplice? Did he drive away with the alleged pair of bloody latex gloves that the Police cannot find? Is there a chance he committed the murder himself and double-crossed his partner leaving her to take the blame? He has already admitted to being in the area that day when he dropped Tanya off. The interior of his taxi cab is immaculate, it has been cleaned very recently. Is he a germophobe or was he destroying DNA and fiber evidence? He also has those lacerations on his hand that look a day old and not three days old as he claims. Bibby is a local, did he have an issue with Sterling? Does Bibby stand to gain anything from Sterling's death?

The next picture Myrtle puts on the board is a bit of a surprise to Zeus. The third suspect is Ms. Claudine. Ms. Claudine has no alibi for the time of the murder. If what Tanya told them today is true, then Ms. Claudine is withholding the fact the Police have arrested her niece. Why is she not taking calls from her niece? Perhaps if Ms. Claudine was home alone she would have taken the call from Tanya. Ms. Claudine lives in that big house in that nice neighborhood, so she must be doing well financially. Why has she not provided her niece with an attorney or posted her bail? Could it be she is trying to protect her social status by not publicly associating with a murder suspect that is also related to her? How much of the whole incident did she really watch from her living room? Could there have been any family drama, how well did they get along? Does Ms. Claudine stand to gain anything from Sterling's death?

The fourth suspect Myrtle puts on the board is Tanisha. Tanisha is Ms. Claudine's daughter. She was in the area because she appeared at the house on the day of the murder. Once again Zeus is surprised by Myrtle's selection. "You're looking at me like, what does this have to do with the price of peanuts, but hear me out", she asks. In Myrtle's mind, Tanisha may have had another reason to be in the house besides comforting her mother. Perhaps she was in the house the whole time. Myrtle made a mental note to log the distance and time it takes to get from the beauty salon to the house. This would not be the first time a family member committed a crime to protect another family member. Could the daughter have been protecting her mother from something or someone? Myrtle's research has not turned up any criminal records for this suspect.

Does Tanisha stand to gain anything from Sterling's death?

Zeus takes a few minutes to examine the new evidence board before playfully remarking, "You have everybody on here except the housekeeper and the gardener." Myrtle is quite prepared for this question, "This is not a case of the Butler did it. The housekeeper left early that day and the gardener had already left by 8:30 am." The alibis have all checked out to her satisfaction. After reviewing Myrtle's updated evidence board Zeus still feels like the strongest evidence points toward Tanya as the murderer. He shares with her that while he recognizes the effort, there is just not enough there to make a strong case for the other potential suspects on the board. "You may have a blind spot when it comes to this young lady", states Zeus. "If you feel too close to her I can assign you to another case." Myrtle tries her best to hide her frustration, but she understands Zeus's response. He is convinced Tanya is guilty and does not see how anybody else could disagree with that. If Myrtle is being honest, she questions it herself, has that last meeting with the accused influenced her approach to the evidence? If Tanya is not the killer, then why does it look like she is? Myrtle knows Zeus is a good officer who follows the law, so she will need to find more evidence.

CHAPTER 19

Myrtle exits the conference room feeling more determined than ever. The Police have twenty-four hours before they have to officially charge Tanya with a crime, and there are still a few hours remaining. Myrtle will not be able to sleep at night if she does not do all that she can to uncover the truth. Murder bugs her, and something about this murder really bugs her. She leaves Zeus at the Police station and heads off on her own to learn more about Bibby, Tanya, Sterling, Ms. Claudine, Tanisha, and the whole family. Zeus has some reports to file and update. He also has leads from another case to follow up on as well. As a consolation to his new Consultant, he promises to call as soon as Sterling's toxicology report from the laboratory is available. Myrtle must decide what the best approach should be going forward, she needs to maximize the few remaining hours. Should she go back to the beginning and talk to people who rode the train with the suspect? The task of trying to track down and interview a bunch of train passengers is daunting. She has taken that train several times, she loves the convenience but hates how people dress. Ms. Jenson is not a fan of this ultra-casual travel dress code that has become so popular. The thought of being exposed to all those pairs of yoga pants and flip flops is enough to make her sick. People used to get dressed up to travel on the train. She longs to be able to travel without being exposed to people's underwear and dirty feet. Myrtle has only lived in Viewgrove for a few years, she has never known a time without the train line. Unfortunately, she does not have any connections at the train station to help narrow her search. This town feels so much like home that at times she must remind herself of how long it has been. Another thought crosses her mind. She could always ask Zeus to get her a list of train passengers from that day, but it may take him some time to go through the proper channels to obtain the information. Time is at a premium right now.

Just then Myrtle has a better idea. Maybe the place to start is with the family. The time has come to elicit help from an old friend. She exits the Police station and makes her way to her car. Myrtle is naturally observant and five minutes into her drive she notices a luxury black sedan in her rear-view mirror. She is not a car expert, but she recognizes it as a foreign model, not something she sees around town every day. A few miles and a few turns later she checks her rear-view mirror again, and there is now a compact light blue vehicle behind her. Twenty minutes later Myrtle arrives at her destination, the Viewgrove Gazette Headquarters. Once parked in the guest lot she makes her way inside.

"Myrtle Jenson to see Davina Roberts please."

While brainstorming, she remembered that Davina's family has lived in town for several generations. Without even looking up, the desk receptionist asks her if she has an appointment? The receptionist is one of those rude types who act like they are bothered that you are making them do some work. Myrtle is unfazed and kindly reminds the receptionist that she is not the one who forced her to fill out an application for that job. "Tell her Myrtle Jenson is here to see her." The desk receptionist releases a deep sigh and slight eye roll before picking up the phone and dialing Davina. Two minutes pass before Ms. Roberts steps off the elevator to greet Myrtle. The two exchange greetings like they are old friends. The reporter appears genuinely happy to see her guest. Davina looks sharp as usual. She is dressed in a beautiful earth-toned floral-print sleeve dress that confirms Ms. Jenson's theory that this lady knows how to dress. It warms her heart to see young women dressed sensibly. This is such a wonderful contrast to the women Myrtle usually sees walking around town in their skimpy clothes with all their personal business on full display. Davina's warm welcome makes Myrtle feel more at ease about asking her for a favor.

They spend a few minutes catching up before Davina's guest tells her why she is there. Myrtle explains how she needs to find out more about Sterling Washington and Ms. Claudine. Ms. Roberts knows from experience that if Myrtle has come to see her then it must be important, and there is probably a good newspaper story in it for her too. She is always conscious of the newspaper's need to increase sales, and the types of stories that might help to do that. The two people that she is being asked about are older than Davina, so she does not

have any firsthand knowledge to share. There is another
way though, she invites Myrtle upstairs to see if there is
anything in the newspaper archives about them. Myrtle is
in search of possible motives or any detail that might help
the pieces they have make some sense. She asks Davina to
pull up what she can regarding any County liens or past
due property taxes, anything that Sterling's life insurance
policy would bail them out of. Davina logs onto the
county real estate website but the information is not up-to-
date. She does not appear discouraged or even surprised.
Reporters are used to overcoming obstacles. She simply
picks up her phone and calls one of her contacts over at
the County Treasurer's office who confirms everything is
current and there are no outstanding liens. The reporter
gets to work on her laptop creating a search for any stories
the newspaper may have published on the family. Unlike
Zeus, she is an expert on the computer, her fingers just
glide over the keyboard. The most recent search result is a
story about Ms. Claudine and Sterling opening a brand-
new upscale beauty salon. "Is this beauty salon still open
today?" asks Myrtle. Davina does not need the internet to
answer that one, "Oh yes, it is doing extremely well too,
they even offer spa treatments by licensed aestheticians."
She offers to print out the address but warns Myrtle that
the services are pricey. "They do high-end work, but it will
cost you." Davina gets a facial treatment there to repair
and rejuvenate her skin anytime she knows she has a big
upcoming television appearance.

"Are there any other articles available?"

Davina's fingers once again tap on the keyboard and the
search continues. There is no shortage of articles detailing

Ms. Claudine's charitable work in the community. Myrtle is embarrassed that she had no idea Ms. Claudine gifts college scholarships to local children, serves on the board of several non-profit organizations, or any of the other charitable acts spotlighted in the articles.

The next search result is a little older than the first one. This article is from the time of the great train crash. The story is about the lawsuit and huge settlement paid out by the railroad company to the victims and families of the victims. There are many articles written around this time about the great train crash, it was a huge event in town. Myrtle would not have chosen to live in Viewgrove if the train line had not been there because it would have been too difficult to travel the country. Long time locals have told her many stories about the tragic train crash. The next article in the search results deals more specifically with the victims. It describes how large settlements were paid out to the families who lost loved ones in the crash. The extreme weather conditions and fire made it very difficult to locate remains. Unfortunately, all the bodies were not accounted for, and payments to these families were put on hold until it could be proven they had died as a result of the crash. A few years passed without any payments made to the families with missing relatives. Finally, a group of families with unaccounted-for loved ones joined together to sue the train company. Eventually, they won their lawsuit and were awarded settlements also. Among the names of the unaccounted for is Tanya Washington. The Reporter turns wide-eyed toward Myrtle for her reaction, "Do you think it's a coincidence?" Myrtle does not believe in coincidences.

Davina is very intrigued by what she is learning and asks if she can continue the research? Myrtle has no objections so long as she is kept informed of whatever is learned about Tanya's family before anything gets published. Davina is a person of her word, so Myrtle has no concerns about agreeing to the arrangement. Sources only provide tips and background on breaking news stories to those they feel are trustworthy. Word-of-mouth travels quickly in Viewgrove. If the word ever got out that Davina is untrustworthy it would be the end of her reporting career in town. Myrtle can clearly see the Reporter is intrigued so she decides to leave her to her research. Davina does not even notice Myrtle stand up to leave. She is embarrassed when she looks up and sees Myrtle with one arm already in her coat sleeve. She jumps up from behind her computer and helps her guest finish putting on her coat while apologizing for being so distracted. "It's quite alright young lady, you continue your research, I can show myself out."

CHAPTER 20

Myrtle is back in her car, and on her way to the next destination. She slows down and pulls out the printout Davina gave her with the building address to the upscale beauty salon. She is reminded of how she really needs to learn to use the GPS directions feature on her phone. As Myrtle slows to read the building numbers, she catches a glimpse of a luxury black sedan in her side-view mirror. The sun casts a long shadow inside the car that makes it impossible to determine who is driving the vehicle. The sedan is two cars behind her. Just then Myrtle spots the sign for the beauty salon but unfortunately, the entrance is on the other side of the street and she cannot get over in time due to traffic. Most of the traffic appears to be for the beauty salon which confirms to her that the business is doing very well. The salon is a beautiful building with a modern architectural design. It stands out because a lot of the business buildings in Viewgrove have renovated interior spaces but maintain the old-style exteriors. The beauty salon has valet parking out in front. Myrtle maneuvers her car around the block and pulls into the line of luxury vehicles waiting to drop their passengers off at the front door. A quick glance in the rear-view mirror confirms the same luxury black sedan is still two cars behind her in the valet line. This is a popular destination, so it could just be a coincidence. The line is moving quickly and there are only two cars ahead of her. The last car ahead of her drives off and it is Myrtle's turn in line. She pulls up to the valet desk and the valet attendant hurries around to the driver side to wait for her to exit and hand her a ticket. Myrtle exits the vehicle and steps into the fall air. Moments after Myrtle's feet hit the asphalt there is the loud sound of tires screeching followed by the sound of an accelerating engine. She turns around just in time to see the black luxury sedan come barreling toward her at full speed.

Myrtle is in trouble, the luxury sedan accelerates so quickly it is on her in seconds flat, all she can do is brace herself for the impact. She is suddenly snatched out of harm's way by a quick-thinking valet attendant who pushes her out of the way of the approaching car. Myrtle is sent rolling across the cold asphalt as the black luxury sedan barely misses its attempt to run her down. It is so close that the corner of Myrtle's purse catches the front corner of the sedan and smashes part of the headlight. The luxury sedan keeps going without even slowing down, its tires screech as it exits the parking lot and races down the street.

Concerned witnesses outside of the beauty salon rush over to help Myrtle and the valet. She opens her eyes slowly to people talking softly over her, asking her name, and if she is okay. She manages to get out a breathy response, "I'm a diamond dear, you can't break me." As soon as Myrtle makes a move to get up she can hear people yelling for her to stay down while they call the paramedics. She quickly regains control of all her senses and assures the concerned crowd that has gathered that she is okay and there is no need for the paramedics. The damage looks worse than it is, Myrtle is lucky the valet pushed her out of the path of the car as quickly as he did. She escapes with some scuffed up clothing and a slightly bruised ego. She has one of the valets to help her to her feet. Another valet helps her to pick up the contents of her purse. The contents of her purse were scattered all over the road among shards of clear plastic from the black sedan's broken front headlight. Thankfully for Myrtle her purse is the only thing that contacted the charging vehicle. Now back on her feet, she scans the scene for her hero valet. Her eyes locate him outstretched on the curb with a small crowd around him. She makes her way gingerly over to him and thanks him for his bravery. He smiles and waves at her to let her know he is okay, but Myrtle can see that his leg is possibly broken. The sedan must have clipped his leg on its way past. She would love to call Zeus and have him pick her up and drive her either home or to the hospital, but now is not the time for that. Her body is bruised but not broken so she pushes on. None of the witnesses she interviews got a good look at the car's license plate number. There is a good chance the plates were either removed or stolen anyway. She is able to get the name of the valet worker, so she can check on him later. The Police will be here soon enough to handle things.

After a few swipes at her clothing to dust herself off Myrtle slips into the beauty salon unnoticed. She is certain the receptionist looked her up and down and made a face. The receptionist is a professional faker who smiles and greets her new guest pleasantly when she approaches. There is no mention of Myrtle's scuffed appearance, instead, she offers a dry, "How's your day going?"

"It was going fine until I had a little car trouble", replies Myrtle.

"I'm sorry to hear that, how can we help you today?"

Myrtle states Sterling Washington had recommended his beautician to her and she would like to schedule an emergency hair appointment. The receptionist has a strange look on her face before kindly explaining that Sterling did not have a beautician in the shop. In Myrtle's opinion it is unlikely Sterling was coloring his own hair, maybe Ms. Claudine's daughter can help with some answers. She then asks to make an appointment with Ms. Claudine's daughter, Tanisha. Ms. Jenson explains that her hair is delicate, and she refuses to have just anybody doing her hair. Sterling had always told her this place was the best, but if that is no longer true please let her know. The receptionist takes a look at Myrtle's hair, roughed up from the street, and it qualifies as an emergency to her. She types some things into the computer before looking back up and informing Myrtle that Tanisha does not have any openings for new customers. To try to keep Myrtle's business she offers to let her watch the beauticians work, enjoy the complimentary coffee, and see if there is another beautician's work that she likes. If she sees somebody she likes, the receptionist will be happy to check their calendar and possibly schedule an appointment. Myrtle enters and is impressed with the interior of the beauty salon, it is absolutely beautiful inside. She selects a seat that will give her the best view of all the beauticians, but more importantly puts her in earshot of most of them. Her plan is to catch up on some beauty shop gossip. Every beautician saw her sitting there but assumed she had an appointment with another beautician. Seeing as Sterling was part owner of the shop, his murder is still probably the topic of discussion today. Perhaps she could even get one of the beauticians to answer some questions. It is not long before she is joined by a curious visitor. "Hi, I'm Arianna", says a young voice. Myrtle glances over at the child addressing her, the girl appears to be around six or seven years old. The child is very friendly and apparently bored of being in the salon because she is talking non-stop. Myrtle wonders where her parents are, and secretly hopes they will be along any minute. A beautician waves and addresses the young girl by name as she walks past. Now that she thinks about it, the child appears very familiar with the surroundings. Myrtle smiles and waves back. The beautician asks if Arianna is bothering her?

"Oh not at all, she's been keeping me company. I'm Myrtle Jenson."

This is the perfect opening to ask about beauty products, hair, and scalp damage. The beautician is more than happy to answer questions about hair. She explains that what Myrtle is describing sounds like an allergic reaction to a chemical, and a licensed beautician would never apply dye unless the condition was cleared up. Myrtle asks if the beautician knew Sterling? The memory causes her to become emotional and teary-eyed. She explains how Sterling used to come in all the time and she would help him look up stuff on the internet. The beautician returns to her waiting client and Myrtle is once again left with a chatty Arianna. Just then Ms. Claudine's daughter, Tanisha, emerges from a back corridor and instantly spots the two of them. She immediately calls her mother, Ms. Claudine, to tell her about what she sees. Tanisha calls her daughter over to get her away from Myrtle, "Arianna, don't you have some homework to do?" The young girl quickly says goodbye and disappears through the back corridor. Tanisha asks Myrtle what she is doing at the salon? Ms. Jenson replies that she is thinking of making an appointment, "Do you have any appointments open?" Tanisha does not feel comfortable with Myrtle hanging around the shop. She swears her staff is booked solid and apologizes for not being able to fit her in. She tells Myrtle if she really needs to get her hair done today, her mother, Ms. Claudine, has agreed to make it up to her. "Your mother does hair?" Tanisha explains that her mother has been a licensed beautician for over thirty years. According to her daughter, Ms. Claudine would love to see her in something else besides grey curls. Myrtle would love an opportunity to ask Ms. Claudine more questions even if it means getting a new hairstyle. She walks back out to the valet and hands them her ticket. The valet worker is surprised to see her, nobody knew where she disappeared to. He informs her the Police are looking to speak with her and hands her the contact card the Officer left. When the valet pulls her car up, she cautiously looks both ways twice before stepping out onto the street.

CHAPTER 21

Ten minutes into the drive and the phone begins to ring loudly. The ringer volume startles Myrtle as the phone bumps around in the car's center counsel. Her phone is normally not out, so the ringtone is set as loud as it will go, so she can hear it when it is buried in her purse. She is famous among her friends for forgetting to charge her phone and often leaves the house with less than thirty percent battery life remaining. It becomes a real nuisance when trying to take group pictures and the phone is dead. In Myrtle's defense, she has only been stuck with a dead phone two, maybe three times tops. On rare occasions, she forgets her phone at home completely. Zeus is constantly fussing at her about keeping a fully charged phone with her for safety when she leaves the house. As a compromise, she bought a car charger, although admittedly she rarely uses it. Today is different though, today she remembers to plug her phone into the car charger. Myrtle's focus is getting to her destination and she is in no mood to allow this caller to distract her. The thought of letting it just go to voicemail crosses her mind. She rationalizes that if it is important they will call back, won't they? Irritated, she glances down only to see Zeus's name on the cell phone caller ID. She had thought maybe it was just one of her girlfriends from water aerobics. If she is being completely honest with herself, she will admit she would rather it is his name flashing across the display. Her girlfriends never want to spend much time discussing the cases she is working on. She had talked herself out of calling Zeus after her accident at the beauty salon, had he heard about it from another officer? The thought of him concerned about her welfare makes her think of them as partners like in a buddy cop series. She hopes Zeus will help her find the owner of that black foreign sedan. The driver handled the vehicle very well, could the black sedan possibly belong to an experienced driver like Bibby? Myrtle's mood lightens up and she presses the answer button on her steering wheel to answer Zeus's call. The car's Bluetooth activates, and his voice flows through the speakers and fills the cabin. The tone of Zeus's voice is all business, this is not a casual call. Myrtle fears something bad has happened since she left him at the Police station earlier. Have the Police decided to officially charge Tanya ahead of the twenty-four-hour window?

"Hello, Myrtle, I just got a call from the Police Chief."

Myrtle is unsure what to make of this news, did Zeus receive a promotion, should she congratulate him or be concerned? She does not have to wait long to find out. Zeus proceeds to detail the nature of the call. The Police Chief called him because he received a call from the

Mayor. The Sterling case has come to the Mayor's attention and he is pressuring the VPD to conclude the investigation. The Mayor has been made aware there is already a suspect in custody, but no formal charges have been filed yet. "Outstanding citizens such as Ms. Claudine deserve our department's best effort", stresses the Police Chief. The Mayor is demanding the VPD end the delay and immediately charge their suspect. He wants the perpetrator prosecuted and the case closed as soon as possible. The Viewgrove Police Department can expect he will be following the case closely going forward, and expecting results. There is an election coming in November and he plans to run as the "low-crime" candidate. It is not good for his campaign to have one of his biggest donors involved in a lengthy murder investigation. The Mayor explains that Ms. Claudine is a friend, and he does not appreciate her, or her family being unnecessarily harassed. Mayor Wilkinson went further by reminding the Police Chief how much money Ms. Claudine has generously gifted to improve the lives of people in town, including the Police department. He would hate to see such an extraordinary citizen's good name and reputation be slandered. It turns out Ms. Claudine filed a complaint with the Mayor's Office about a reporter asking a lot of questions, and also an investigator visiting her businesses and frightening off customers. "I don't suppose you would know anything about that would you?", asks Zeus. Without even waiting for an answer he continues. He is pretty sure he already knows the answer. On second thought he does not even want to know, he would rather retain his plausible deniability. "I appreciate how hard you're working on this case Myrtle, but I need you to steer clear of Ms. Claudine and her family."

A knot begins to form in the pit of her stomach as the guilt starts to weigh on Myrtle's conscious. She feels conflicted, does she tell Zeus she is headed to Ms. Claudine's house right now? She certainly does not want to go against his wishes, but she feels if she has more time at that house she can solve this case. Myrtle is aware there is a very real chance the decision to go to Ms. Claudine's house may result in being fired as a Police Consultant. What should she do? The mystery solver in her says she should continue to the house, she was invited after all. However, it is doubtful Zeus will see it her way. Myrtle needs a minute to weigh her options, she already has a strike against her today. The pain from the fall at the salon starts to return, letting her know the painkillers are wearing off. She pulls over into the parking lot of a strip mall to take more aspirin. Myrtle would give anything to lay her aching body on her couch right now and watch classic television. A long soak in her bathtub would do her body wonders. In the strip mall is a dry-cleaning business displaying a huge sign promising garment cleaning in one hour. Perhaps this is an opportunity to kill two birds with one stone. She can get the road marks out of her jacket, and it will give her mind a much-needed distraction. Myrtle walks into the dry-cleaning business to get an opinion on whether it is even possible to remove these road marks? It cannot hurt to ask even though the damage to the garment may be permanent. Myrtle removes her jacket and hands it to the attendant to examine. Without a change of clothes, the attendant will have to make a visual assessment of their customer's remaining garments while they are still being worn. The attendant excuses herself and carries the jacket to the back of the store, presumably to ask a more seasoned dry cleaner. While waiting, Myrtle passes the time by reading the advertisements posted on the walls of the business. There is one poster that catches her eye, and initially, she does not know why? The advertisement is for a new stain removal process that promises incredible just-like-new results. The attendant re-emerges from the back of the store with the jacket and a big smile on her face. To Myrtle's delight, the attendant feels quite confident all the scuffs can be removed.

"That's great news, you wouldn't believe what kind of day I've had."

"We can have it done for you in an hour", advises the attendant.

"Just like new?", asks Myrtle while pointing to the poster on the wall.

The attendant nods her head up and down while preparing a dry-cleaning ticket, "Just like new." She is pleased to know the advertisement is working and more than happy to explain how well the process works. The attendant explains how this is their newest process, she just hung the poster on the wall today. Myrtle compliments her on how well the poster is put together. The attendant is flattered and excitedly reveals that they use actual customer garments on all their posters because they feel it makes them more believable. "How do the customers feel about their garments being used in advertising?" According to the attendant, a lot of the customers enjoy seeing their garment on the wall. This way the customers know these are real situations and not just stock pictures from the internet. The small print on the ticket and on the wall says the dry cleaner is free to use pictures of customer garments for promotional purposes. The garment in the new poster was brought in just yesterday and was able to be completed in an hour. The attendant explains how this customer cut themselves while chopping some vegetables from their garden. This new cleaning process removed every stain and left the garment looking just like new. Myrtle thanks the attendant and puts the dry-cleaning ticket in her purse. The short walk back to the car is less painful thanks to the aspirin. The time has come to make the decision to either proceed to Ms. Claudine's house or return to the Police Station.

Myrtle telephones the Police station looking for Zeus but is informed he is in a meeting. The young officer on the phone is very friendly and asks if he can help. Myrtle explains to him that she would like to watch the interview tapes with Tanya again and could she pick them up later? "Pick them up?", asks the young officer. "No offense, but what kind of cell phone do you own?" Myrtle pulls her face back from the phone to look at the manufacturer name before providing it to the officer and hoping that she is correct. She is relieved when the young officer knows exactly what she is talking about. "You don't have to come into the station ma'am, I can just text you the password and you can download what you need from the cloud." Viewgrove PD is trying to move away from paper and compact disk storage and file everything digitally on the shared server or in the cloud.

CHAPTER 22

Myrtle's car rolls up the driveway to Ms. Claudine's house. She must admit it is a beautiful estate, even though she is seeing it for the second time it is still impressive. This is her first time seeing the house without the yellow Police crime scene tape, squad cars, and evidence markers. She reaches the end of the long driveway and puts the car in park. Upon exiting the vehicle, she observes Ms. Claudine standing on the porch waving her over. Unlike Myrtle, Ms. Claudine had no doubt Myrtle was coming over. Ms. Jenson exits her car and presses the lock button on her key. The car beeps and flashes to indicate the doors are now locked. Ms. Claudine seems amused by watching this. As her guest approaches she shouts out to her that she does not have to lock her doors. "You're perfectly safe out here, I leave my keys in my car and I've never had a problem", adds Ms. Claudine. Myrtle smiles to herself as she imagines Zeus's reaction would be to hearing that statement, "He would absolutely lose his mind for sure." She makes her way up the porch steps and is now within a few feet of her welcoming host. Ms. Claudine greets her houseguest with a friendly hello and welcomes her into her home. "Where is your coat?", exclaims Ms. Claudine, "Quick, come in, it's chilly out there." What a difference from the last time the two of them were together. This must be the difference between dropping by unannounced with the Police and being invited over. Right away, Ms. Claudine apologizes for not being able to accommodate Myrtle at the beauty salon. She guarantees she will make it up to her and assures her she is in good hands.

"I promise to take care of you."

"As long as it's no trouble", answers Myrtle.

"Oh it's no trouble, it will be my pleasure."

The interior of the home is as beautifully decorated as the exterior. The room furnishings compliment the colonial style of the property. The Colonial style is a little formal for Myrtle's taste, but she can appreciate it for what it is. She can appreciate most furniture styles although Country, floral print, and white painted wood are just not her thing. Given a choice she prefers a more comfortable look, and this Colonial style furniture looks too nice to sit on, let alone stretch out and binge-watch television with a giant bowl of popcorn. The parlor room reminds her of growing up in a house where nobody is allowed in the living room. The room was like a museum exhibit, look but do not touch. If her mother ever caught her sitting on the living room furniture there would be big trouble.

"You have a beautiful home."

"Thank you, would you like a quick tour?"

Myrtle cannot resist taking Ms. Claudine up on her offer to tour the residence. How could she not be interested to see what the rest of the place looks like, plus it would only be polite.

The gracious Host leads the tour through her house pointing out various design themes, furnishings, and other interesting facts about each room. Most of the commentary is lost on Myrtle because she is too busy trying to figure out how the murderer gained access to the house. This personal tour is so much better than the 2-D room sketches in the Police case file. In her mind, she is matching the Police report to the home layout details of the rooms on the tour. Ms. Claudine does not show every single room but does include a home theater, an office, a bowling alley, and some guest bedrooms. What is most interesting to Myrtle is the tour of the kitchen and the back door that leads to the garden. Ms. Claudine leads her guest to the last stop on the tour, she proudly opens the door to reveal the space. Myrtle is genuinely impressed by what she sees. There is a full-service beauty salon set up in her home. It is comparable to professional basketball players who have full-length basketball courts in their backyards. Being that her host is retired, Myrtle expects to see aged beauty equipment and dated décor, but she is wrong. The shop is immaculate and stocked with the most modern hair dryers and equipment available. Ms. Claudine invites her guest to take a seat while she puts the coffee pot on. 'Putting the coffee pot on' is more of an expression because the shop is equipped with one of those coffee cup machines. Minutes later a coffee cup is being filled with the hot brew. The aroma of fresh coffee brewing fills the salon.

"How do you take your coffee?"

"Sweetener and half-n-half creamer please."

Ms. Claudine hands Myrtle the coffee as she informs her it is going to take a few minutes to set up her hair station. "Please make yourself comfortable, I won't be long", she adds while reaching for the plum stylist apron hanging from a brass hook on the wall. Ms. Claudine disappears into a supply closet and can be heard humming to herself as she gathers her hair supplies. It is clear she loves being a hairdresser because she seems happy and at home in this beauty salon space. Myrtle takes a few sips of the hot coffee, it tastes good since she has not been able to have coffee on her new health program.

While waiting in the salon chair Myrtle passes the time by checking emails on her phone. A check of her text messages reveals the password for the interview videos, just as the young officer promised. Myrtle takes a moment to marvel at modern technology and makes a mental note to thank the young officer the next time she is at the Police Station. Thank goodness there is strong service available in this salon because she would never ask her host to use her WIFI network. She downloads the first video and fasts forward through the less interesting parts. Ms. Claudine catches a glimpse of Myrtle's phone and asks if she is watching one of those reality tv shows? "Oh no, nothing like that", she assures her before changing the subject.

"I met your granddaughter, she is lovely. Does your

whole family live in town?"

"Thank you! Yes, I'm not aware of any relatives that don't live in Viewgrove."

Myrtle finds the response interesting considering Tanya says this is her aunt. Her host does not care to elaborate so Myrtle changes the subject again. "I stopped at that Dry Cleaner up the road, have you tried them?" Ms. Claudine is unsure of the place Myrtle is referring to, "I don't know, my housekeeper handles my dry cleaning, I'm unsure where she goes." Myrtle responds with an acknowledging nod but adds, "That must be why the attendant was so excited when a local celebrity came in. You'd never believe what they brought in." Ms. Claudine is not interested in local gossip. She ignores the last question and asks her guest to move over to the wash station where she places a protective vinyl cape around her. Myrtle pauses the video long enough to send a quick text to the reporter, Davina Roberts, to let her know the Mayor wants the case dropped. Davina texts back a few of the details she has uncovered and the two of them agree to meet later to discuss the matter further. Behind her, the streams of water can be heard bouncing off the white ceramic sink as her host runs her hand under the streams to check the temperature.

It appears everything is ready, so instead of putting her phone back in her purse, Myrtle simply holds it under the black shampoo cape. She leans back in the chair and Ms. Claudine begins to run the warm water through her hair. Just then her cell phone starts ringing loudly. The first thought is to let it all go to voicemail and check it after her hair is done. The first call is ignored and goes to voicemail but then the phone immediately starts ringing again. Whomever this is must really need to get in contact with her. Finally, she decides to find out who it is. She asks Ms. Claudine to pause while she sits up in the chair and checks her missed calls. The missed calls are from Zeus and he has also left a message. He must have another development in the case. This is one time she wished Zeus knew how to text. She is tempted to try to text him but concedes it is easier to call him back. He types so slowly it would take too long to exchange lengthy text messages.

"Is everything okay?", asks a concerned Ms. Claudine.

"It's fine. Do you mind if I use your restroom?"

"Sure, it's right through there, first door on the left."

Myrtle is really excusing herself for some privacy while she calls Zeus back. Even though it is just the two of them in the shop, she locks the door behind her before calling him back.

Zeus answers his phone on the first ring. "I'm glad you called me back." He cuts right to it and explains the toxicology report is back, and it reveals traces of poison in Sterling's blood stream. Myrtle is confused as to how the poison was introduced into his system, because there were no puncture marks on his hands, arms, or neck. It is quite possible a puncture mark was missed. The body will have to be checked again. This time they have something new to look for. Just then it hits Myrtle, and she suddenly realizes how the murder was committed.

"Come and pick me up from Ms. Claudine's house right away, I know who killed Sterling!"

"What are you doing at Ms. Claudine's house, I told you to avoid contact with her?"

"I'll explain when you get here, please hurry?"

It does not feel like she has been in the bathroom for a long time, but perhaps she has because she hears knocking. It is Ms. Claudine knocking on the bathroom door. "Is everything okay in there?" The concerned host listens at the door for a response. Myrtle runs the water and washes her hands while yelling back through the door that she will be out in a minute. When she comes out of the bathroom Ms. Claudine is waiting over by the wash station with her protective plum apron and black latex gloves on.

"All right, are we ready? Just lay back right here."

"I'm sorry, I completely forgot about an appointment, I must be going", blurts out Myrtle.

Ms. Claudine tries to persuade her to stay by pointing out her hair is already wet, so she might as well stay long enough to finish the wash and set. She insists the coloring will not take more than a few minutes. Despite Ms. Claudine's best efforts Myrtle's mind cannot be changed. She thanks her host for the hospitality as she hastily gathers her purse and heads toward the exit. "I'll show myself out, thank you for the coffee." Before Ms. Claudine has a chance to launch another protest, Myrtle is through the salon doors and looking for the way out. In her haste, she gets turned around and heads the wrong way. This is her first time in this part of the house, it was not part of the tour, and it is a little confusing. Myrtle is down her second corridor before she realizes she is headed in the wrong direction. She will have to turn around and go back. Ms. Jenson retraces her steps all the way back to the front room where she runs back into Ms. Claudine. Her host, still wearing the plum apron, is blocking the front door with a knife in her hand and a menacing look in her eyes.

"You've figured it out, haven't you?"

"What do you mean?" asks a nervous Myrtle as her mind searches for an escape.

"You really should have dropped the case as the Mayor told you to."

"Nobody tells me what to do, I do a little thing called, WHAT I WANT", retorts Myrtle.

CHAPTER 23

Myrtle is trapped in a serious predicament and feeling quite vulnerable. The painkillers she took early are due to wear off any minute and leave her with diminished mobility. She could try to make a run for the back door, but it is most likely locked. Is there any chance she can get it unlocked before her knife-wielding host catches up with her? Ms. Claudine waves the knife in the direction Myrtle just came from, motioning for her to head back to the beauty salon. Myrtle puts her palms up in a defensive position and tries to reason with her.

"Think this over Ms. Claudine, you won't get away with this."

"Oh, yes I will. I caught you trespassing and was forced to defend myself."

Myrtle makes a run for the kitchen door but is swiftly cut off by Ms. Claudine. That old beautician is faster than she looks. She barely escapes a knife gash by ducking behind the kitchen island. The situation has turned volatile, and that dash for the door took a lot out of her. Myrtle attempts to put some space between them but for every step back she takes, Ms. Claudine takes one forward. She starts pushing over end tables and anything within reach that can be pushed between them as an obstacle. Just then the doorbell rings. "It's the Police!", screams Myrtle as loud as she can. It is a desperate attempt to bluff her attacker and make her reconsider coming after her. Neither one of them knows who is really at the door. All Myrtle knows is if she heads back down into that beauty salon she is not coming out alive. Regrettably, Ms. Claudine believes she is bluffing and continues advancing toward her. The doorbell rings again. Myrtle yells for help but when there is no response she worries it is a delivery person, and not the Police. Just as her attacker charges again, Zeus bursts through the front door. The loud crash stuns everybody. As soon as Ms. Claudine realizes it is Zeus she drops the knife and starts thanking him. "Thank goodness you showed up Detective, I caught this intruder breaking into my home!" Zeus orders everybody to freeze while he evaluates the situation. He looks around the disheveled room, and then at Myrtle standing there out of breath with wet hair, and wearing a shampoo cape. "What's going on here?" He orders them both to stand and face opposite walls while he kicks the dropped knife out of reach. The concerned Detective looks over and asks the lady if she is okay?

"I'm okay. I feel so violated, Detective, I want her arrested immediately!"

"I was talking to Myrtle", answers Zeus.

There is no mistaking the outrage plastered across Ms. Claudine's face. If looks could kill, the Detective would be dead where he stood. Myrtle's response is five simple words, "I know who killed Sterling!" Now that the adrenaline is wearing off, Myrtle realizes she must look a hot mess, and is immediately embarrassed that thought crossed her mind.

Zeus radios for backup, and a few minutes later the driveway is full of Police cars. The Detective asks for an explanation on who killed Sterling? Myrtle begins by explaining how according to the people she spoke to at the beauty salon, Sterling had been feeling guilty in his old age. As it turns out, he and Ms. Claudine had cheated his niece out of her inheritance. They had both built a living off what was supposed to be hers. According to Davina's research, Sterling and Ms. Claudine were part of the group that sued the rail company for unaccounted bodies after the great train crash. "It is my belief that they knew she was alive the whole time and fraudulently claimed the money for themselves." The inheritance Tanya keeps referring to in her interviews is actually a settlement. Sterling had been trying to get Ms. Claudine to come clean for years. Her daughter now runs the businesses and partakes in the profits. Ms. Claudine is more interested in continuing her lifestyle and passing the wealth down to her own kids. Myrtle shares the story she learned on her trip to the salon earlier. "On a trip to their salon, Sterling notices one of the young beauticians surfing the internet on their smartphone and strikes up a conversation with her. He asks her if she can look up people in other cities on her cell phone? He asks for help searching online for his missing niece who left Viewgrove on the train years ago.

Sterling offers to pay for any information she finds but she must keep it between them. Every time he would visit the shop he would get an update. He knows he cannot have the young lady call the house without Ms. Claudine becoming suspicious. When the young lady starts to make progress, he starts requesting to visit the beauty shop more often for updates. Sterling did not drive, so Ms. Claudine would be the one to take him to the salon." Myrtle theorizes that Ms. Claudine probably started getting suspicious of all these trips to the salon. "She is a former beautician and starts to offer to dye Sterling's hair under the guise of saving time. In reality, she is adding a toxin to the hair dye to make him weak and homebound. Soon Sterling is too weak to travel to the beauty salon or make any requests of anybody."

"That's a ridiculous accusation!" protests Ms. Claudine.

"Oh, you can drop the innocent act", replies Myrtle.

"As Sterling becomes weaker, Ms. Claudine starts to make up excuses for why she cannot take him to the beauty salon on the days he asks. Sterling must have figured out something was going on. On what turns out to be his last visit to the beauty salon he learns that his long-lost niece has been searching for him too. This is the best news he has heard in years. On the anniversary of his brother's death, he contacts his niece and invites her to come and see him. All he will tell her is that she has an inheritance due to her and he is sorry. Sterling was never able to make it back to the beauty shop again, but every day he would insist on sitting out on the porch and hope that his niece arrives."

"On the day his niece arrives Ms. Claudine freaks out. Her first thought is to scare the girl away, but what if she comes back? Then as the girl is balled up in the corner passed out, she has another idea. This idea will solve all her problems and kill two birds with one stone. She can silence Sterling, get rid of the niece, and keep all the money. Some items from the house were planted in Tanya's suitcase to frame her to make it look like a robbery gone bad." Ms. Claudine is livid over what she is hearing.

"This is all lies! Any fool can see that it was a robbery gone bad."

"The Police found stolen items in the murder's suitcase!" barks Ms. Claudine.

"That they did, the same stolen items you planted there for them to find."

"Detective, I'd like to file a complaint against this Myrtle woman!"

"Over the years Ms. Claudine has become accustomed to living a certain lifestyle and she is not about to let that change now. She solves her growing issue by stabbing Sterling and framing Tanya. The grief Ms. Claudine expressed when Detective Chaplin informed her about her cousin's death was real. She was truly sad that her cousin had passed away. Whether she meant to kill him or just injure him is unclear at this point. Either way, she is responsible for Sterling's death."

"Ms. Claudine Davis, you're under arrest for the murder of Sterling Washington."

Zeus orders Officer Leighson to arrest her and read her rights. Ms. Claudine protests the arrest and especially being handcuffed. The Officer must tell her twice before she complies. She cannot believe what is happening right now and keeps looking around for somebody to put a stop to it. Her mood quickly shifts from panic to anger. The anger is accompanied by several violent outbursts.

"You're going to hear from my lawyers!"

"My good friend the Mayor will hear about this!"

"I'll sue the whole department!"

Myrtle surmises Ms. Claudine is the one that called the Mayor's Office to try and get the investigation shut down. A wry smile comes across Ms. Claudine's face as she reminds Myrtle that she is a close friend of the Mayor and is a huge contributor to his campaign. She boasts she is too important to go to jail. "By the time my lawyers get done with you two the only jobs you'll be able to get will be sweeping up hair in my beauty salon." Zeus has heard enough and motions for Officer Leighson to transport her to the Police Station for processing. The Detective escorts a relieved Myrtle to his car, he will assign an officer to bring her car back to the station. He advises her there will be more questions about what happened at the house and what evidence she may have uncovered.

CHAPTER 24

The car ride back to the Police Station is a quiet one. Myrtle is unnerved by today's events but is not physically harmed in any way. It is not every day that somebody tries to kill you, that is not something you just shake off. She is used to solving cases from the safety of the Jury Box, and did not envision getting so physically involved when she agreed to the consulting job. Zeus did not intend for her to come this close to danger either, and feels guilty that she had to go through the experience. He pulls into the parking lot and gives his passenger a few minutes to gather herself before entering the station. The pain and stiffness from the fall at the salon have returned to Myrtle's body, so she is moving a lot slower. She needs to find more aspirin to take. A few more moments in the car and she pushes herself to go. At Myrtle's request, the two of them pay Tanya a visit. Tanya is anxious to hear what the two of them have to say, she is hopeful that it is good news about her case. Zeus starts the conversation by offering to get her something to drink, coffee, soda, or water? Tanya gladly accepts his offer and asks for a diet soda with a cup. In her mind, if they are offering her beverages then this must either be a friendly interview, or they need something from her and are buttering her up. Myrtle returns with the diet soda and foam cup, carefully placing it exactly in front of their interviewee. Tanya eagerly accepts the beverage and pulls the tab open with her right thumb. She covertly attempts to wipe any prints she may have left on the can as she pours the liquid into the cup. Myrtle can only shake her head, obviously Tanya watches too many Police television shows.

Zeus informs Tanya they have brought her aunt into the station for questioning. If there is anything else she needs to tell them about the case, he suggests she does so now. The news is met with a little confusion, but she does not appear overly concerned. If anything, Tanya appears buoyed by the news. Myrtle is the next person to speak, "Detective, the good news is I don't believe Tanya killed Sterling. The bad news is I don't believe this is Tanya." Zeus looks over, the look on his face says that he was not expecting this revelation. If this is not Ms. Claudine's niece, then who do they have in custody? Myrtle cuts the suspense short and explains that Davina's research proves this lady is not whom she claims to be. A small fact that surfaced during Davina's research is that Tanya is left-handed. Once Myrtle reviewed the interview video on her phone she knew. In the interview tape, the subject used her right hand to accept beverages and to sign her written statements. Just moments ago, she used her right hand to pop open the tab on the soda can. Not to mention the old expired identification she was carrying when she was arrested, clearly, this was to conceal her identity for as long as possible. Tanya stares at the table the whole time Myrtle is talking. Zeus stares at her expecting her to deny all these claims, but she does not. The denial never comes, she does not even lift her eyes to meet Myrtle's. She seems resigned to her fate. There is no need to continue the charade any longer, the best option now is to come clean.

Tanya eventually lifts her head to face her interviewers. She takes a long sip of her soda, then proceeds to tell a story that has them both captivated. Myrtle is right, her real name is Tiffany Johnson. Tanya was her best friend and eventual roommate. They met on the train years ago while both running away from Viewgrove, and quickly became the best of friends. They were two young girls tired of living in a small town. Although they were each leaving for different reasons they bonded over their shared desire to start new lives somewhere else. "Tanya legally changed her last name soon after she moved out of town. She wrote Ms. Claudine and Sterling a letter when we reached our new town and told them she had left, but more importantly had survived the train crash. Although she was excited to start a new life she did not want the family in Viewgrove to worry. She viewed the great train crash as symbolic of her new start, she was burning her old life and starting a new one." Life was great for several years, they both established careers and new friends. Most of the people in their circle did not even know they had ever lived in Viewgrove. However, the good times did not last forever. Unfortunately, Tanya fell on hard times after being diagnosed with a terminal illness. Her beautiful twisted locks fell out and she became too weak to work. She sold all her worldly possessions to pay for treatment and to qualify for government assistance.

Tiffany invited her to move in with her toward the end just to cut expenses. Tanya was too ashamed to ask for any financial help from the extended family after having no contact with them for so many years.

"I tried to convince her to reach out to her family, I practically begged her."

No matter how much Tiffany pleaded Tanya would always answer by saying, "She'll think about it."

Eventually, Tanya got too sick to travel and passed away three months later. "She was the type of person to give you her last dollar, her last days should have been more comfortable than they were." While going through her deceased friend's effects, Tiffany came across the old correspondence from all those years ago. It took her a whole year to decide whether to contact any of Tanya's family. Did they even know she had passed away? Eventually, she decided to reach out to them even if it meant opening a painful memory. It seems like everybody is on social media, so one day she took a chance and looked to see if she could find any of the people named in the old letters. As luck would have it she found both Ms. Claudine's and Sterling's profiles. To increase her chances of getting a response she sent them both messages pretending to be Tanya. Ms. Claudine did not respond but Sterling did. She doubts if they would have responded if they knew it was her. During the exchanges, Sterling invited her to Viewgrove and told her about an inheritance. Tiffany did some research on what Sterling may be referring to and the more she found out the angrier she became. It was then that she hatched her plan to travel back to her hometown. The family in Viewgrove had not seen Tanya in years. Tiffany was counting on them being so glad Tanya was home they would hardly question if it is really her. Even if they did, she still had the information she had uncovered, and they probably would not want the bad press that would follow if the information is ever made public. Tiffany was determined to get what she felt was rightfully owed to her dear friend Tanya.

"What were you going to do with the money?" asks Myrtle out of curiosity.

Tiffany admits she did not know? She thought maybe buy a headstone for the gravesite, pay off the medical expenses, or donate the rest to Tanya's favorite charities. From how Tanya described her family, Tiffany did not expect them to split their fortune with her. She really expected them to offer her a quick payoff in exchange for never coming back to town.

CHAPTER 25

Myrtle wakes up the next day at her usual time, around six o'clock in the morning. She takes a long hot bath to help her wake up, but more importantly to soothe those muscles that still ache from the events of the past two days. After getting dressed she goes over her schedule for the day, while simultaneously preparing her fruit and vegetable smoothie. She watches the blender pulverize the ingredients, and wonders how long she can stay on this healthy program? A calendar notification flashes across her cell phone to remind her she is meeting with Zeus today to discuss the Sterling case. So much happened yesterday so Myrtle is anxious to speak with him. However, that conversation will have to wait because right now it is time for Myrtle's hair appointment. Traffic is light, so she arrives at her regular hair dresser's salon early. Her hairdresser is surprised that she has made an appointment before she is due, some clients get their weeks mixed up but never this one. Myrtle explains that she believes her hair was just possibly washed with a toxic serum, but she cannot be sure. The hairdresser feels a little unqualified after hearing the story.

"Are you sure you don't want a doctor to look at it?"

"You are my hair doctor", answers Myrtle.

"Just let me know if you notice anything out of the ordinary on my scalp."

Myrtle's hair appointment concludes without incident. Her hairdresser does not believe there are any toxins in Myrtle's hair but still feels she should see a doctor. So much for Ms. Claudine's plans to give her a new hairstyle and color. She struts out of the salon looking and feeling like herself again. By the time the hair appointment is over it is time to meet with Zeus. There is not enough time to go all the way home again. Fortunately, the locations are not too far apart.

As Myrtle pulls up to the agreed-upon meeting place, she spots Zeus's car already parked in the lot. She is a few minutes early but he has still managed to beat her there. The few extra minutes are spent conducting the customary check of her face and hair in the sun visor's vanity mirror before going inside. The door chimes announce to everybody inside that somebody new has entered the building. Zeus offers up a big welcoming wave from where he is seated. Myrtle always sleeps better when a case is solved, and she considers it a good sign that Zeus appears to be in a good mood. They exchange greetings as Myrtle places her purse down and slides into the vacant booth bench opposite Zeus. The Detective starts off by complimenting Myrtle's hair.

"Thank you. It was a mess the last time you saw it!"

Davina Robert's article on Sterling's murder appears in the morning edition of the Viewgrove Gazette. There on the front page of the Gazette in big bold letters is the article titled, 'The Thief's Gift'. The story lays out the details of the Sterling case and challenges the readers to consider how somebody who has gifted so much to the town could also steal from it. Does someone's good deeds ever outweigh the bad? Zeus was reading the story while waiting for Myrtle to arrive. He asks if she has read the article yet? It is possible Davina provided her with an advanced copy. To his surprise, Myrtle has not had a chance to read the story yet. Zeus figures Myrtle is anxious to hear about the developments in the case, so he gets right to it. He confirms that Ms. Claudine has been formally charged with Sterling's murder. He is curious why Myrtle even suspected her when all the evidence pointed at Tiffany? Myrtle admits she really did not consider Ms. Claudine that strongly until the day they went to visit her for the interview. "The lady did not tell you she witnessed the murder the first time you spoke to her but volunteered it the second time." Why would she ask how Sterling is if she witnessed him being stabbed? Also, she thought it was odd that Ms. Claudine did not mention the phone calls she was getting from Tiffany at the Police Station. "It could be the calls slipped her mind initially, but she got a call while we were right there, and she still said nothing." The second clue did not reveal itself until much later. Myrtle states she had come to a dead end with trying to find evidence to link Ms. Claudine to the murder. Then while she was at the dry cleaners she happened to see a poster on the wall. The poster was for a new cleaning method and featured a luxury robe. "The same robe Ms. Claudine was wearing the day we dropped in on her unexpectantly for that interview." The chatty clerk at the dry cleaners confirmed to Myrtle that Ms. Claudine brought the plush robe in herself, he remembered because the housekeeper usually drops off the dry cleaning. The robe had blood stains which the clerk said was from Ms. Claudine cutting herself while chopping vegetables. Myrtle releases a deep sigh, she really hates she did not get the chance to ask Ms. Claudine where she got the robe from.

"That was a great tip and it paid off", adds Zeus.

Zeus reveals the Police search of Ms. Claudine's house led to them finding the dry-cleaned bathrobe in her closet. When the sleeves are sprayed with a solution and placed under the violet-blue light it reveals blood splatter. The lab is running tests, but it will be a surprise if it does not test positive for Sterling's blood.

"That dry clean attendant Ms. Claudine tipped to keep his mouth shut owes her that $100 back.", adds Myrtle.

The Police search of Ms. Claudine's personal salon uncovers a case of discontinued hair dye with a bottle missing, and another bottle open and almost empty. Further research reveals this dye was discontinued over twenty years ago because it was determined to be poisonous when combined with conditioners. It was manufactured overseas but popular because it was cheap. Apparently, this is what caused the scarring on Sterling's scalp, it is a rare reaction. The hair solution seeps into the scalp and causes side-effects. The most common side-effects are muscle weakness, fatigue, and loss of motor functions with prolonged use. Users complained of feeling heavily sedated and unable to recognize when they had seriously injured themselves. Most new beauticians have never even heard of the product. The product was not available to the public, buyers needed a professional license to purchase it. Any beautician in possession of it was required to return all unopened and opened boxes for a full refund.

The Police Laboratory speculates prolonged exposure to the dye may have caused Ms. Claudine to act irrationally. The dye was outlawed over twenty years ago due to these type of side-effects. Ms. Claudine told the medical evaluators that the voices in her head made her do it. Just like one of those pharmaceutical commercials on television, the possible side-effects for this product include paranoia, hostility, and hallucinations. The batch that Ms. Claudine had has been sitting for twenty years making the formula extremely potent. Her high-priced attorney is suggesting she is not mentally fit to stand trial. Zeus states he is pushing to have Ms. Claudine charged with not only Sterling's murder but the attempted murder of Myrtle too. It will be a fight to have her declared mentally competent. To think Ms. Claudine could have resolved the situation with a quick payoff and gone on living her comfortable life. She wanted desperately to keep Sterling quiet and from ruining everything for her and her kids. "If humans were meant to be controlled they would have come with remotes", quips Myrtle. Just then she remembers that she drank the coffee in Ms. Claudine's home salon and asks if the coffee was tested? She did not feel sick now, but she would like to be sure in case she develops some symptoms down the line. Zeus is tempted to keep her guessing, but he puts her mind at ease by assuring her the coffee was tested and there was nothing dangerous found. Zeus believes Ms. Claudine intended to derail the investigation and keep Myrtle quiet by poisoning her with the hair dye and not the coffee. He does believe the Police will be able to place her in the black sedan that tried to run Myrtle over. A big black luxury sedan with tinted windows was discovered under a black tarp parked in one of the garages on the property. It has damage to the front end that matches the accident scene outside of the beauty salon. "One thing I don't understand is why the valets at the Beauty Salon did not recognize the black sedan?", wonders Zeus. The Department of Motor Vehicles shows the car is registered in Sterling's name. Myrtle theorizes that even though the black sedan belonged to Sterling he probably had not driven it in years.

"I really wished you would have called the Police with your suspicion instead of going out to the salon or house. Once she realized you had figured it out she could not let you leave."

"I had to be sure before I accused her. I didn't want to smear the name of a prominent member of the community and cause you to get into deeper trouble with the Mayor", confesses Myrtle.

Myrtle is curious about what is going to happen to Tanya, aka Tiffany? Zeus expects to see Tiffany's charges reduced from attempted murder to possibly intent to commit financial fraud through identity theft or obstruction of justice or something. It is not up to him, but he figures she will get a lighter sentence. With a lesser charge, perhaps the judge will grant her shorter jail time or possibly probation. It all depends on how the judge views it and on whether she has a prior history of breaking the law. The Police still must confirm this new identity she has given them. "I still can't believe we were talking to the roommate the whole time", admits Zeus. "Don't beat yourself up Detective, even salt looks like sugar from the right distance", offers an empathetic Myrtle. "I don't get this lady", starts Zeus, "Even after she is arrested, Tiffany never accuses Ms. Claudine of the murder?" Myrtle thought that was odd as well until she learned Tiffany was not really the niece, so she had no legal claim to any money. "Ms. Claudine in jail would make it almost impossible for Tiffany to get a payoff because she needed to avoid any legal processes." With both Sterling and Ms. Claudine out of the picture Tiffany would be forced to deal with the daughter who has less of a connection to Tanya.

There is something else Zeus has been wondering about, and now that the case is over he feels okay bringing it up. "I've been meaning to ask you, what did you whisper into Sterling's ear on that first day?" Myrtle leans in as if telling a secret.

"I introduced myself, said it was an honor to meet him, and then I promised to find out who killed him."

The Detective is happy to be wrapping up this case, and also relieved nobody else was seriously injured. He is so glad he called Myrtle in to consult on this case. "So," begins Zeus, "Is there any particular reason you chose this place for us to meet?" A wry smile spreads across Myrtle's lips as she watches him trying to piece it together. Zeus had forgotten all about their bet over the existence of the taxi driver, but she had not. "This is Anna's Diner Detective, they have the best sundaes in Viewgrove." Once Myrtle mentions sundaes it all comes back to Zeus's memory and all he can do is throw his head back and smile. Myrtle smiles too as it is clear he has finally caught on.

"You didn't think I would forget, did you?", asks Myrtle rhetorically.

"Are you always this sassy?"

"Not always, sometimes I'm sleeping."

A waitress walks over to their booth, so they mute their conversation until after she leaves with their order. Zeus had originally planned to speak to Myrtle about whether she still wants to continue as a Police Consultant. After this case, he believes Myrtle is very capable of taking care of herself. If she decides she no longer wants to work with the Police, he is sure she will let him know. He was going to mention how he is considering retirement, but he changes his mind after they start talking. If he does retire he hopes she will continue the help the Police with cases. All of this is a conversation for another day. Right now, Zeus decides to just enjoy the moment and the upcoming sundaes. "Ooh here come the sundaes", points out Myrtle excitingly, "You're in for a real treat Detective!"

The End.

ABOUT THE AUTHOR

M. Malenga is an independent writer who lives and works in the United States. He is the author of Riddle of Darkness: A Myrtle Jenson Mystery. His advice for writers young and old is to keep writing. "Never be limited by other people's limited imaginations" ~ Dr. Mae Jemison.